Moriarty's Men

BOOK FOUR

# THE VALLEY OF FLAMES

## EVA CHASE

# CHAPTER ONE

*Jemma*

The hotel suite was perfectly still, perfectly silent. As it should be, considering I'd booked every room on this floor, the one below, and the one above, and left strict instructions that staff were to stay clear unless called for. Ensuring that level of service and discretion hadn't been cheap, but what had I spent all this time building my wealth for if not this moment?

This moment when I might not only get to avenge my sister but also save her.

The posh Tokyo executive hotel held all dark wood, black leather, and tan walls, soothingly refined. It was almost a shame pushing all the living room furniture off to the sides in a jumble to clear the densely woven carpet in the middle.

Bash let out a grunt as he heaved the sofa the rest of the way over, the ample muscles in his shoulders bulging. My right-hand man eyed the space we'd opened up skeptically. "Are you sure you wouldn't be more comfortable on the bed?"

"The point isn't for me to be *comfortable*." I gave the coffee table one last shove for good measure. "Ideally my body should remain on as level a surface as possible. Even a firm mattress will have some give. Anyway, I won't be conscious to care. Why shouldn't you have a proper place to sleep?"

Bash's expression turned even more incredulous when he raised his light green eyes to stare at me. "As if I'm going to sleep while you're wandering around in whatever hell those monsters live in."

"It might take me a while," I said. "You'll need to rest sometime. Besides, if something goes wrong for me, there won't be anything you can do about it. I'll be fighting my own battles. Your most important job is making sure no one disturbs me on this plane of existence."

"And reapply the dressing you talked about as necessary."

I shrugged. "It'll fade slowly. Maybe you shouldn't take a full nine hours all at once, but a few hours won't be critical. The ceremonial preparations are complicated to set up, but once they're in place, there's not much else to do."

Satisfied with the state of the room, I went back to the laptop I'd left open on the marble counter in the kitchenette to check the courier's website. "All we need is for that last delivery to get to us… And it should be here within the hour, or someone will be getting a phone call they won't enjoy."

"I'm sure it'll turn up." Bash sat himself down on one of the stools along the counter and ran his hand over the black stubble shading his tan scalp. He nodded to the computer. "Have you looked up the UK news to see—"

"No," I said, cutting him off. "I know what I intended. I don't need some outside account of the incident."

If my plans in Scotland hadn't fulfilled my intentions accurately, I couldn't do anything about that fact now. What happened to Sherlock and the rest of the London trio—the three crime-fighters I'd somehow ended up letting into my life, my mission, and to some extent my heart—didn't matter anymore. It *couldn't* matter, not when Olivia's life might hang in the balance.

I'd failed my little sister once before. I'd thought she'd died because I hadn't come back for her at our family's commune quickly enough, because I hadn't been able to escape with her in the first place. She'd deserved so much better... She deserved every particle of attention and concern I had in me until I brought her safely home.

My tongue slid against the backs of my teeth with the urge to suck on a sugar cube. The sweetness might have brought a tiny bit of comfort, but I didn't know how it might affect the ceremony ahead.

"How are you going to look for your sister once you're in that place?" Bash asked. "You're going to be on their turf—what's to stop them from capturing you however they captured her?"

"I'll figure it out once I'm there. She's my sister—we have a connection. It shouldn't be too difficult." I hoped. I'd never ventured into the realm of the shrouded folk before, and the few respected cult elders who'd gotten to make that journey once or twice had stayed tight-lipped about their exclusive experience. I didn't know what the place even looked like.

To tell the truth, I wasn't entirely certain that the ritual I was preparing was a perfect match for the ones I'd witnessed parts of in childhood. It'd been a long time. If my memory had failed me, I'd just have to track down some cult member who could give me the proper instructions with the right motivation.

"And the rules the shrouded folk follow when it comes to human beings should still apply whatever plane we're on," I added. "They can attack me, but they can't lay any claim over my soul without my agreement."

Bash grimaced. "And I'm supposed to be okay with the idea of them attacking you?"

I gave him a fond if slightly exasperated look. The ex-military sniper turned hitman had been my closest companion for the last several years—employee, friend, and recently lover. Though we didn't talk about feelings often, I knew how deep his devotion to me ran. Since our relationship had taken a more intimate turn, though, this protective streak had been coming out more and more often.

"You should know better than anyone that I can defend myself just fine," I said.

"These creatures don't fight fair."

"And neither do I." I reached out to grasp his hand on the countertop. "I know the idea of all these supernatural horrors is pretty new for you. I know you'd come with me, guns blazing, if you could. But I need you here, and I know these fiends well enough to maneuver around them. I won't be looking for a fight. As soon as I've got my sister, I'm getting out of there as quickly as I can."

"I'll do everything you've asked me to do," Bash muttered. "I still don't like that you have to take this step at all."

"But I do have to. You *understand* that, don't you?" I squeezed his fingers. "You took a big risk to save your younger siblings way back when. And they weren't in anywhere near the kind of danger Olivia is. She must have already endured so much... I can't leave her in their clutches one second longer than I can avoid."

Bash's face tensed. For a second I was worried I'd managed to offend him by mentioning his younger brother and sister. It'd been a rare moment of openness when he'd told me about how he'd brought them to live with their grandparents away from their abusive dad when he was only thirteen. He didn't generally like to talk about his childhood.

He exhaled slowly and shifted into his Shakespeare-quoting voice with its hint of irony. "'Truth is truth to the end of reckoning.' You've got me there."

"Imagine what the Bard would have made of this storyline."

"It'd have given him plenty of material, that's for sure." Bash managed a smile. "I'm still hoping it'll turn out to be a comedy rather than a tragedy."

"Well, there's not much the shrouded folk hate more than being laughed at."

Bash's phone vibrated in his pocket with a faint hum. He took it out. "Yes, he can come on up." His amusement faded as he put the phone away. "That last delivery is here."

My pulse skipped a beat. For all I'd talked to him with total confidence, I was nervous about this trip too. But there was no delaying it.

I shut the laptop. "I'll get the rest of the supplies."

As Bash accepted the box from the delivery guy at the door, I spread a spotless white sheet on the living room floor. Then I turned the air conditioning up so the suite would be appropriately cool by the time everything else was ready.

Bash brought the box over to the kitchen. I'd already gotten out a large glass serving bowl. I plopped in the softened beeswax and hemp oil I'd already acquired, tossed in a baggie of lavender, and dug into the box for the other herbs that would go into this concoction.

The final mixture let off a pungent, almost chemical smell as I mashed the dried leaves into the waxy oil with a pestle. The scent brought me back more than a decade to watching the elders prepare an honoree for the journey to the realm of the fiends they all worshipped. The man had swayed in the erratic movements meant to honor the shrouded folk, a dreamy smile on his face, as if he couldn't imagine anything more wonderful than visiting the source of the monsters that demanded blood and devoured children's souls.

I would have been one of those childhood sacrifices if I hadn't made a side deal to allow my escape. I had no idea how the shrouded folk had ended up taking Olivia. Fifteen was their preferred age to fully enjoy the energy we gave off, and she'd have only been thirteen when I'd come back three years later to rescue her. I'd always assumed the fiend who'd been eyeing me had devoured her early out of anger at my disappearance. But the shrouded one who'd brought me evidence that she was still alive had said she'd been "taken but not consumed."

They'd played that card to stop my efforts at destroying their base of human support in this world. I still intended to see them cut off from humankind if I possibly could. But I had to get Olivia back first, so that she didn't pay for my defiance any more than she already had.

I added a little more of a couple of the herbs until I felt I'd gotten the balance just right. Then I scooped about half of the mixture into another bowl and put the original one into the fridge.

"You have the pills?" I said, even though I'd already double-checked a couple hours ago.

Bash patted his shirt pocket. "Right here."

"I need to shower, and then we can get started."

I washed every inch of my body and hair with a bar of plain soap and rinsed myself thoroughly with cool water. My hair still hung damp against my shoulders when I came back into the living room naked. The broad windows on either side of the southeastern corner were bare, letting in all the sun, but I'd chosen this suite specifically because there was no neighboring building tall enough to look straight inside. If someone farther afield took a gander with binoculars, they'd get an interesting show.

Bash's gaze traveled over my body, leaving a tingle of heat in its wake. I knew how good his body could feel against mine, but that was one more distraction I had to put out of my head.

I brought the bowl of herbs, wax, and oil over to the sheet and knelt down on it. With broad swipes, I smeared the mixture into the fabric. Then I painted my skin with it, starting with my feet and working my way up. Bash took a glob to coat my back, his touch steady but gentle.

The cool air chilled my damp skin. I worked the paste into my hair and then finally wiped it across my face, not sparing even my eyelids or my lips. The pungent stink clogged my nose. My stomach lurched, and I swallowed down the bile that started to rise up my throat.

"You'll know the effect is fading if you can see spots of bare skin on my face or arms," I said. "The sheet will stop the rest from evaporating. When you notice any skin that's not shiny with the mixture anymore, just dab some of the leftovers in the fridge there."

"Now you take the pill and that's it?" Bash said.

"Everything we've done sets the atmosphere. As I go into the trance, I'll focus my mind on the shrouded folk. That should take me past the final hurdle."

I held out my hand, and he gave me the pill. It was so small I could swallow it without any water. Then I sat down on the sheet and began to methodically fold it around my legs and torso, with a twist here and a contrasting angle there, leaving no pattern to the creases. The shrouded folk abhorred any kind of mathematical arrangement.

By the time I reached my shoulders, the pill's effects were seeping through my mind. My thoughts were fogging, drifting aimlessly and colliding at random. I lay back with my head to the brightest strip of sunlight and closed my eyes.

"I'll be back as soon as I can," I managed to mumble.

My awareness of the room faded away into the haze of the drug and the herbal stench flooding my lungs. I drew up memory after memory of the commune I'd grown up in, the ashy rotten scent of the shrouded folk, the boy I'd seen them ravage in a blaze of light—on and on, sinking deeper and deeper into each moment—

With a lurch, my consciousness plunged down into a thicker darkness. My lips parted with a scream that didn't make it past my throat. Light flared through my closed eyelids, and my back hit solid ground with a jolt that radiated along my spine. The herbal smell fell away, replaced by that familiar odor of desiccated rot.

My breath caught in my throat as I warily opened my eyes. I'd arrived in the realm of the shrouded folk.

# CHAPTER TWO

*Bash*

As a man of action, watching the woman I loved lying pale and motionless on the floor, knowing she was facing the most difficult trial of her life and not being able to lift a finger to help her—there was no word for it other than "agony."

I had a clear view of Jemma's whole sheet-wrapped body where I'd stationed myself on the sofa. For the first hour after she'd faded away, I hadn't been able to do much more than mark each shallow breath. They came so far apart, no more than a few each minute, and with so little rise to her chest, it'd have been easy to mistake her for dead. The greenish pallor her herbal concoction had given to her face and arms only added to that impression.

It took all my self-control not to prowl around her as if that would protect her more than I already was, or worse, to try to shake her awake. To see those brilliant gray eyes gleaming at me the way they were meant to. To know the demonic creatures she was tangling with hadn't wrenched her away from me.

She'd said it could take days. I was starting to wonder how *I* was going to survive that long.

After a while, I forced myself to go over to the kitchen counter. I could still keep an eye on her for any sudden changes from the stool there, but poking away at the computer might make the time pass faster.

I meant to use that time somewhat productively, checking up on her various business ventures and looking into arrangements for other equipment we might need. If she came out of that hellish realm with her sister—no, *when* she did, I corrected myself; this was Jemma Moriarty I was thinking about—I had to assume we'd continue our campaign against the communes that allowed the shrouded folk access to the human world in the first place.

Instead, my fingers took on a mind of their own and typed the name "Sherlock Holmes" into the search field.

Unsurprisingly, a major incident involving one of the world's foremost criminal investigators hadn't gone unreported. Several pages of results came up discussing the "horrific fall" or in one case where the headline writer got a little too clever with his alliteration, the "tragic tumble" of London's famous consulting detective. I clicked through to a couple articles that looked less on the sensationalistic side.

It appeared Sherlock's colleagues had remained tight-lipped. Even though they knew perfectly well who'd pushed the man down that cliff, the articles didn't make any reference to Jemma, only noted that investigations were in progress. When it came to the detective himself, the reports were similarly vague. He was in a Scottish hospital receiving "the highest standard of care," but no one seemed to know how critical his condition was or whether his life was on the line.

He couldn't have been feeling too spry after that fall, no matter how Jemma had positioned it.

The lack of news wasn't exactly satisfying. I skimmed through a few more accounts before accepting I wasn't finding out any more than that, and then gave up.

My fingers hovered over the keyboard for a few seconds in indecision. Jemma's comment from this morning had been running through my mind ever since she'd made it. She was off attempting to rescue her little sister. Maybe that made this the perfect time to check in on my own family.

I didn't search for information on my siblings very often. Even from afar, even just observing through a computer screen, I couldn't quite shake the sense that the life I'd made for myself might somehow tarnish theirs.

Seventeen years ago, when I'd gotten them out of our parents' house, I'd been a hero to them. That was the last time I'd seen them face-to-face. Since then, I'd become a killer and a criminal. I'd made the choices that had felt right to me in the moment, and I wouldn't have traded my partnership with Jemma for anything, but no one would have looked at me and seen anything but a villain now.

They were doing well for themselves, as far as I could tell from the public record. My brother Samuel had become manager of the hardware store he worked at. A couple weeks ago, he'd completed a marathon. It looked as though he was still with the same girlfriend who'd been showing up next to him in social media photographs for a few years now.

My sister Charlotte had finished her MA in social

work this past spring. She was already knee-deep in initiatives to support abused children. Children like the kid she'd been. Now *that* was a real hero.

I considered her in the slightly out-of-focus photo, her black hair falling in tight braids around her smiling face, and tried to picture how she'd react to seeing me again. Even without knowing what I'd been through and what I'd done, I had no illusions about myself. Something would show in my expressions, in the way I carried myself. You couldn't hide certain types of history.

Would she see the big brother who'd saved her... or a man with too many similarities to the aggressive pricks she was fighting now? I was nothing like our father, but most ordinary people wouldn't differentiate between the varying ways we used violence to accomplish our ends.

The tension that had already been churning in my stomach expanded. I shut the laptop and pushed it away.

I did eventually need to eat something, or I wouldn't be much use to Jemma when she actually needed me. We had supplies for when she came to that would do in a pinch, but I'd rather not make any more noise in here than I needed to. Instead, I went down to a room on the floor beneath our main base of operations at the opposite end of the building, so there'd be as little chance as possible of the sound disturbing her, and ordered room service.

To my surprise, the concierge with whom Jemma had made the arrangements for our stay brought the cart up rather than one of the regular restaurant staff. He lingered in the hall after he'd set the tray with my meal on the room's table. His head dipped in a quick bow.

"If there's anything else I can do for you or your

associate, please let me know. I hope your other colleagues have not run into any issues?"

I guessed I couldn't blame him for wondering where the hell the other people who should be occupying all the rooms we'd booked were. But we'd picked this city partly because the Japanese were a lot less likely to really pry than if we'd found some spot in, say, America.

"We have some setting up to do," I said vaguely. "No problems at all. If there's anything else we need, we'll be sure to let you know."

He bobbed his head again and slipped away. As long as we weren't disturbing any other guests or making an obvious mess, I doubted he'd intrude.

As soon as he'd disappeared into the elevator, I carried my meal up the other room. Seeing Jemma in her prone state took away any hunger that might have developed at the rich smell of the curried beef. I forced the food down as quickly as I could.

The sun was starting to sink low on the other side of the hotel. I walked into the waning light streaking through the windows to study Jemma up close.

Her concoction still shone on her face and her arms where she'd crossed them over the folds of the sheet. Her eyelids didn't so much as twitch. I suspected if I reached down, she'd be cold to the touch. With the way she'd cranked the air conditioning, I'd had to put on a sweater to avoid being chilled.

As I turned to go back to the sofa, the air between the living room and the kitchenette rippled with a wavering light. I froze, my hand leaping instinctively to the gun tucked into my jeans, but in a matter of seconds it was obvious a gun wasn't going to do anything against this uninvited visitor.

The strange light shifted into a more defined form: a humanoid figure wrapped in strips of thin, bleached fabric, only fathomless shadow where a face should have been. It didn't completely solidify but kept a filmy quality, the edge of the counter showing through its body.

I let my hand drop from the gun, but my nerves stayed on high alert. I'd never seen one of Jemma's monsters as anything more than a flash or a blur before, but I recognized it from her descriptions. I was staring at one of the shrouded folk.

One of the fiends she was attempting to trounce on their own territory right now.

A thin, faintly rotten scent tickled my nose. I folded my arms over my chest, staying between Jemma and the thing, and scowled. "Get the hell out of here. You've got no business with us."

The creature's voice came out in a dull rasp. "I wouldn't be so sure about that."

"You're not even supposed to be showing yourself to me, are you? How many rules are you breaking right now?"

"Exceptions may be made." The shrouded one drifted a foot closer, and my stance tensed all over again. If Jemma had been wearing that protective cuff of hers—but she couldn't have slipped into the shrouded realm while she was shielded from them.

They'd attacked her before when she'd broken her contract with the one monster. Was this thing going to make another go of that?

If it did, how the fuck could I stop it?

Jemma had talked about mathematical patterns repulsing the fiends. If worst came to worst, I guessed I could start shouting out my times tables.

"I repeat, get the hell out," I said in as threatening a voice as I could muster. I didn't want to make any literal threats in case those turned out to be only a bluff.

The shrouded one turned its shadowy "face" toward me. "The bloodling that was ours isn't here."

Couldn't it see Jemma lying in the living room? Or—could it only identify her from its sense of her spirit, the part of her that had traveled across the realms? A flicker of relief ran through me.

"No," I said. "She isn't. And I'm not going to give you anything."

"She is acting against us again. We warned her."

"She isn't touching your precious communes. That was the deal you made with her—leave them alone, and you'd leave her sister alone."

The fabric strips billowed farther out, and the scent of it thickened. "Where has she gone without you, then?"

As if I'd tell it. "If she wants you to know, she'll pass on the message."

It was silent for a long moment. The sense prickled over my skin that it was studying me. Then it said, in the same dull voice, "You could save her."

The prickling shot straight through my chest with a jolt of anxiety. "Save her from what?"

"She is walking a dangerous road. Do you really think she can challenge all of us and survive? But perhaps if you offered yourself in exchange, whatever she is attempting, we will let her return unharmed."

"You'd make a contract with me, huh?" I said with purposeful skepticism, but my heart had leapt. I'd always known I might die at Jemma's side. If I could give my life to ensure she kept hers, even if it was in a deal with some monster rather than a bullet I hadn't dodged, I'd take that offer without hesitation.

"Exactly. What do you think, bloodling? Are you her champion or are you not?"

The question raised my hackles, but I kept my mouth shut. Its use of the term "bloodling" only emphasized the unearthliness of the creature in front of me.

Jemma had warned me, not that long ago, never to negotiate with the shrouded folk. Not to believe anything they said or offered. No matter what they proposed, they would twist a situation to their own interests.

I wanted to fight for her, fight alongside her. I didn't want to risk giving my life up for nothing. Maybe I'd dealt with all kinds of human garbage over the years, but I had to admit I didn't know how to read the creature in front of me.

Jemma wouldn't want me to agree to anything this thing suggested. If I was acting *for* her, the only thing I could do was refuse, no matter how much I wished there really was some way I could ensure her safety.

"Her champion commits only to her," I said firmly. "I'm not drawing up any contracts with you or your friends. So I'll tell you one more time—get out of here."

"You can always change your mind," the shrouded one murmured, but it did, finally, fade away.

The hairs on the back of my neck still stood on end. I wasn't even sure the thing had left or whether it might be watching me unseen. Fucking freaks.

My fingers itched to assemble one of Jemma's spiral sequences on the nearby surfaces, but I didn't know if that would disrupt her journey, and besides, I had no idea how to construct one properly. As I hesitated, another thought popped into my head.

Mathematical patterns. Order and rhythm. Like the beats of Shakespearean dialogue, set to his favorite iambic pentameter.

A small smile crossed my lips. I wasn't sure this would have much effect, but it'd make me feel better doing *something*, anyway.

The bedroom's TV offered a wide selection of on-demand movies. I scanned through them until I found one of the more faithful Shakespearean adaptations. With a click, I set it playing, leaving the volume high enough to be audible but not so loud it would reach all the way to the living room.

Let's see if the fiends wanted to pay any more calls while the Bard's poetry filled the air.

# CHAPTER THREE

*Sherlock*

Waking up to the bright lights and insistent beep of a hospital room was becoming an uncomfortably familiar experience. I furrowed my brow at the stark white ceiling above me, crisply clean air filling my nose, and shifted on the firm mattress.

John's face jerked into view in an instant, his eyes wide and his mouth flying open with a hasty, "Stay still."

By the time he'd given the warning, I'd already determined its validity for myself. The second I'd adjusted my position, a flare of pain had shot down my back, up my neck, and through my shoulders as well. I clenched my teeth against the dull throbbing that continued to radiate through my body like an echo.

I could take stock to some extent while lying prone. Though sore, my awareness reached every part of my body —nothing was numbed or paralyzed. A more distant ache surrounded my right forearm, which was encased in a cast from the hand to just above the elbow. I'd been attached to a dispenser of some sort of painkiller, but one obviously not strong enough to completely offset my injuries.

Injuries. Because I wasn't here through my own imprudence this time. I'd been… walking along a mountain path with Jemma. She'd wanted to show me something. That was the most recent memory I could dredge up, and the edges of it were blurred.

"Sherlock?" John said tentatively, and it occurred to me that given the state of my body, he might have significant concerns about my mind.

"I believe that is still my name, unless someone has changed it on me," I said. Talking set off a small but sharp jabbing through my ribs. I took a slow breath before continuing. "How long have I been unconscious?"

Relief loosened only a little of the worry on my friend and partner's face. "Two days. They kept you in an induced coma for the first stretch until they were sure they'd treated all your injuries."

Another voice carried from farther across the room—the low, blunt tone characteristic of Detective Inspector Garrett Lestrade. "You survived that murder attempt rather well, all things considered. The fractured arm was the worst of it." He stepped forward to come into view, his boyish face darkened by a stormy expression.

"Murder attempt," I repeated. Was that really what had happened? The words didn't sound right.

"How much do you remember?" John asked in his gentle way. It wasn't hard to see how he'd done well with his patients before the war had left him too shaky for a surgeon's work.

I frowned. "Walking in the mountains. Jemma said there was something important I should see. The rest…"

"She shoved you off the path down a cliff," Garrett

broke in when I trailed off. "As casual as anything, like she pushed people to their doom every other day." Beneath the hostility in his voice, I caught a note of confusion. Which was understandable, because that was the primary emotion his suggestion stirred up in me.

"Jemma Moriarty tried to kill me," I said, trying out the words. They jostled loose a few more pieces of memory. A hand on my back, a heave of propulsion. A flash of panic as I'd stumbled forward, my feet losing purchase as the ground slanted sharply downward. The thought that I might be about to die.

I'd been careless. I'd assumed Jemma posed no threat, and so I hadn't been keeping a particularly close eye on her movements, despite the precariousness of the path.

On the other hand… I glanced down at my aching but intact body again with a renewed wave of resistance to the idea. Jemma Moriarty might have remained a mystery in certain ways, but I'd come to know her quite well during the time we'd spent together. There'd been no denying how brilliant she was, how skilled at strategizing, at times to the point of topping my own considerable abilities. Nor had she made any secret of how ruthless she was willing to be if the situation called for it.

If the woman had truly wanted to kill me, surely I would be dead? It seemed to me it'd take an enormous amount of luck for even an amateur to fail to cause fatal damage with that kind of fall, and Jemma was anything but.

"We both saw it," John said. He rested his hand on my unbroken arm. "If we'd been closer, maybe we could have caught her—but our first priority had to be getting you help as quickly as possible, of course."

"Of course." Another source of confusion prodded

me. "How did the two of you happen to be there? Jemma made a point of wanting to discuss the supposed matter of concern with me alone before bringing anyone else into it." I'd made no mention of the journey I was taking with her to either of my colleagues when I'd left the hotel.

Garrett paced out of my range of sight and back into it. "Moran came and got us, told us Jemma had been acting strange, that he was worried about what she might do. He drove us out there. And then disappeared after he saw what she'd done—couldn't stick around to deal with the consequences."

"He went with her." The answer was perfectly obvious to me. As was the flaw in his story. "Jemma's man—the man who was ready to kill us on her behalf mere weeks ago, who has shown nothing but total devotion to her—supposedly became so concerned about her apparent instability that he turned to the two of you rather than addressing it with her?"

John's mouth opened and closed again. A look of consternation came over his face. "It did seem odd. But he was insistent about it, and he did take us to her and you, and it's a good thing he did."

"Yes. For me and for her."

"What's that supposed to mean?" Garrett demanded.

I balked at saying more just yet. The theory was only starting to coalesce in my head. I preferred not to make definitive statements until I'd examined all the evidence and drawn more certain conclusions.

I moved my good hand along the mattress and carefully leveraged myself into a sitting position. A fresh throbbing spread through my torso, but it wasn't as debilitating when I was prepared for it. John made a sound of protest that I ignored. I might not always treat my body with the respect he felt it was due, but I did know its limits better than anyone else.

"I need to see the spot where I fell," I said.

Garrett stared at me. "You want to go mountain climbing two days after you fell down a cliff?"

"I want to understand how I came to fall down that cliff and end up in this particular state."

"Sherlock…" John's fingers slid up my arm to grasp my elbow. He looked at me with so much distress and fond regard that my mind, still slightly muddled by the effects of whatever medication the doctors had me on, wandered back to the last moment his lips had pressed against mine.

Something in our partnership had shifted under Jemma's guidance. I couldn't say she'd produced emotions that hadn't been there before, but she'd compelled a desire for each other into the light alongside the desire all three of us had come to feel for her. It wasn't yet clear to me exactly what John and I were becoming beyond friends and partners in our work, but I couldn't deny we *were* more than that now. Perhaps that was why his distress trickled into me. But that didn't change my objective.

"There is more to this scenario than we can comprehend from your panicked observations and my unprepared senses, both viewed through a medium as unreliable as memory," I said. "Unless there's some reason to think I'll injure myself more by taking a car ride and a careful walk out to the spot, with as much assistance as you feel you need to provide, I'd like to resolve that uncertainty as soon as possible. Bring the doctor here if you must. I'll put the matter to him."

"Stubborn as a mule," Garrett muttered, but when he paced the room again, there was more energy to his movements. He was equally eager at the thought of taking action.

From what I'd observed of the three of us, he'd fallen for Jemma the hardest and fastest. Affairs of the heart were hardly my forte. I had no idea what distress Garrett must be feeling, not only at seeing a colleague laid low but at having witnessed his lover committing what by all appearances had been a terrible crime.

John sighed. "Fine. I'll call the doctor. But in my professional opinion, a mountainside is the last place you should be right now."

It took nearly a day longer than I'd hoped, but by the next morning I'd negotiated my way back to the cliff where Jemma had arranged my literal downfall. John helped me out of the car, his expression all disapproval, but he held out his arm to take some of my weight all the same, leaning a little on his walking stick on the other side.

"I'm only coming with you because I know you'll insist on making the walk on your own if I don't," he informed me.

"Noted." Twinges of pain still ran up my legs and through my back, but my resolve to pick apart this mystery was far stronger than any physical malady. I'd swallowed a couple of painkillers in the car a half an hour ago, and their effects were dulling the discomfort without intruding too much on my mental processes.

Garrett came up to support me on my other side, and we began our slow, shuffling ascent of the path, punctuated by the rapping of John's stick.

Something twisted in my chest thinking back to the

first time I'd made this trek, to the gravity in Jemma's demeanor that she hadn't been able to entirely disguise. Maybe she hadn't been trying to disguise it, knowing I'd assume it was related to what she'd supposedly meant to show me rather than a treacherous act she was planning.

She hadn't taken her action lightly, whatever her intent had been. I should have seen—if I'd been paying better attention…

I *had* been charting our progress up the mountain with some focus, in case it would prove relevant to her concern. I spotted the point where she'd asked me to stop and peer down the cliffside before the others needed to identify it.

"Here," I said, nodding to it. We came to a halt on the path right where the faint scuffing revealed the skidding of my feet three days past. I peered down the cliff. The uncertainty I'd felt faded away as the final pieces of evidence snapped into place.

I motioned to my colleagues. "What do you see below us?"

"A whole lot of rock ready to bash your head in, that you were lucky to avoid," Garrett said.

"What else?"

John picked up the thread. "A few small trees, a clump of shrubs—that's where you landed." He pointed to a small cluster of bushes, their wiry branches snapped here and there where I must have collided with them, some fifty feet down the steep incline.

"And what do you make of that?" I asked.

"Like Garrett said, you were incredibly lucky."

I turned to John and raised my eyebrows. "In all our dealings with Miss Moriarty, how often has luck been a deciding factor in the outcome of her schemes?"

He paused. "Well, not often, but why on earth would she shove you down a cliff at all if she didn't want you dead or close to it?"

"That is an important question, but one I think we've already seen the answer to in our own history."

I swept my hand to indicate various parts of the slope. "Look at the terrain. There, the drop becomes nearly sheer with nothing at all to break a fall until you hit the rocky outcropping much farther down. On that side, there are the trees, but they're at least as likely to bash a head as any rock is. A little farther along, there are a few more shrubs, but the terrain there is more uneven, with more loose stones scattered—more chance that a fall will veer in an unexpected direction or a protruding object will cause major damage."

Garrett knit his brow as he studied the landscape. "Where are you going with this?"

"Isn't it obvious? This is the only spot along this path where the drop *could* have been fatal, but isn't because of the precise combination of features. She told me to stop here specifically. A few feet to the right or left, and I most likely would have died. You can't tell me Jemma didn't realize that. But she didn't want me dead." I wet my lips. "She only wanted me—and you—to *think* she wanted me dead."

"There's no way she could have been sure the fall would have followed that exact course," John protested.

"No. It was a risk. She likely expected I'd have been more injured than I was—luck did give me a small bit of help. I don't think she'd have wanted me returning here and making this observation any time soon."

Garrett's eyes had widened. He cursed under his breath. "Bloody hell. She *asked* Moran to get us out here as witnesses—she knew how it would look—she wanted us convinced she'd taken up the villain mantle again too. Why the hell would she go that far?" His voice had gone raw.

The truth of it had already solidified in my head, crystal clear. The twisting in my gut tightened into a series of knots.

"We can't know the full story until we find her," I said. "We need to start tracing her travels from here immediately."

John clasped my shoulder. "Hold on. Even if she didn't mean to *kill* you, she still hurt you. She could do it again. We can't go rushing after her when we have no idea—"

"We do have an idea," I interrupted, more sharply than I'd intended. John's flinch made me wince inside in turn, but I soldiered on. "That's exactly how she wanted us to be thinking so that we wouldn't follow her, at least not in time. But if she wanted me dead, I'd be dead. No, she's gone off on her own again to see out some dangerous mission—something she felt would put us in far more danger than tumbling down a cliff. This was her way of *protecting* us. Of protecting me."

I hesitated, my throat constricting. "She did it because she believed she needed to. Because I proved myself too vulnerable. She didn't believe she could count on me to continue the fight."

Out of the three of us, I'd let the shrouded folk influence me the most. I'd let their shadowy compulsions drive me to overdosing on cocaine in a fit of desperation. If I hadn't—if I'd held steady in the face of their machinations—perhaps Jemma would have welcomed my assistance instead of taking this extreme step to ensure I stayed out of her next plans.

John could obviously follow my line of thinking. He gave my shoulder a gentle shake, the sun in his blond hair and glinting off his hazel eyes giving him an almost cherubic appearance.

"You were up against an unfamiliar enemy with powers beyond comprehension," he said. "No one would fault you for struggling. We *all* struggled."

Garrett nodded, a hint of shame crossing his face.

"It doesn't matter now." I drew myself straighter. "She needed our help even when she fled before. She may very well need it again, considering the creatures we're up against. We *have* to find her, and quickly—and hope it's not already too late."

John inhaled raggedly, and I met his eyes. He didn't have to speak for me to know what he was thinking.

He'd been afraid he'd lost me twice in as many weeks. The thought of racing into similar danger all over again terrified him. Not for himself—John rarely met a spot of danger that didn't exhilarate him. *He* wanted to protect me too.

I didn't know what to do with that urge of his. It warmed me and exasperated me at the same time, and I couldn't logically explain the first reaction. I wasn't sure if acknowledging the concern I saw in him would make the situation easier or harder.

Nothing in my vast range of experience and learning had prepared me for being the most important figure in any other person's life.

I reached for the right words to say and closed on nothing. He made no attempt to argue, though. He knew me, through and through. He knew when I'd made up my mind about a course of action.

I lifted my hand to touch his arm in an attempt at reassurance, and his gaze twitched with surprise. "I'll steer far away from both mountainsides and stimulants this time," I promised. "Your medical skills will be wholly unnecessary when it comes to me."

The words came out awkwardly, but they appeared to land well enough. John's mouth curved with a small but genuine smile.

"Then I suppose we'd better find out what trouble our wayward criminal genius has gotten herself into now, hadn't we?"

# CHAPTER FOUR

*Jemma*

In my first glimpse of the shrouded realm, everything blurred together into a haze of dim gray. I cautiously pushed myself upright on the hard ground, its texture gritty beneath my bare hands. A faint impression of the sheet I'd wrapped myself in had come with me, swaths of it floating around my torso and legs, though it had the same filmy quality that the shrouded folk displayed in the human world. My body was faintly translucent too.

My immediate surroundings looked like a desert lit by moonlight: cracked dry ground with no sign of vegetation other than a few shriveled, leafless shrubs, the impression of a reflected glow streaming down from above. When I peered up at the sky, which was the same dull gray shade as everything else around me, I couldn't make out the source of that pale light. It appeared to spread from one horizon to the other without ever intensifying.

No wonder the shrouded folk coveted our sun if this

was the most illumination they got here. I wondered where they'd developed a taste for that kind of energy in the first place.

A breeze stirred around me, carrying a warbled sound mixed with random clicks and hums. The erratic quality of it set my nerves on edge in an instant. The shrouded folk thrived on dissonance and disorder. I could only imagine how many I'd piss off if I started drawing out Fibonacci sequences here.

The stretch of flat ground I'd landed on ended some fifty feet away with a sprawl of structures that looked half disintegrated—miniature skyscrapers with crumbling roofs and walls, smaller buildings that might only have come up to my knees or my waist that were pocked with craters, all of them leached of any color. As I stared at the apparent wreckage, a prickle of recognition ran up my back.

If I ignored the size and the disastrous state of the buildings… that looked almost like the Tokyo skyline.

I glanced around to make sure I didn't have any company and stood up. Better to get out of this open area before any of the fiends did come wandering this way. I wasn't sure how they'd react to seeing an uninvited human in their midst or how much they could hurt me before I could wrench myself back into my natural realm, but I wasn't keen to find out the answer to either question.

When I approached the ruined city, the similarities to the one I'd left in my world stood out even more sharply. It *was* a sort of shrunken, fallen version of Tokyo. The buildings that would have been dozens of stories tall in reality stood only ten or twenty feet high here. One or two I could have stepped inside through gaping holes in the walls, but no doorway could have fit me. The "roads" were barely wide enough for me to squeeze along—where there was any need to squeeze. In many places the buildings alongside them were little more than scattered rubble.

The sight made my skin crawl. Obviously the state of this replica hadn't affected the actual city in any significant way. The buildings I saw ruined were standing just fine back in my realm. But what kind of warped alien place was this? Had the shrouded folk constructed these models and ruined them out of spite? Had they risen up naturally through some sort of parallel-universe connection? Both possibilities were equally unnerving.

As I picked my way through the bizarre city, the wavering sounds rose and fell around me with no sense of rhythm. The hairs on the back of my neck rose. At a shiver of movement between the buildings ahead of me, I jerked back behind one of the shrunken skyscrapers.

A shrouded one came into view farther down the street, its form more solid here than they ever appeared in the human world. Even at a distance, the pale strips floating around its body looked even more like swaths of dead skin rather than the fabric I'd wanted to think they were. I restrained a shudder. Just when I'd thought the creatures couldn't get any more disgusting.

Thankfully, it wasn't traveling my way. It drifted on past the nearby structures without a sound or any clue as to its purpose here. I waited another few minutes before I ventured farther, keeping my eyes even more carefully peeled for others.

Because this Tokyo was several orders of magnitude smaller than the one I'd left—and for the most part lacking in suburbs—crossing it only took a short hike.

When I reached the fringes of the city and my temporary shelter, I hesitated, scanning my surroundings up ahead.

Another long, flat plain stretched out directly ahead of me. To my left, I spotted a dense cluster of high-rises I suspected must be Osaka. Which would mean I'd originally landed at the edge of the Pacific Ocean, and the expanse ahead of me would represent the Sea of Japan.

The world map unfurled in my mind's eye. If I kept walking straight ahead, I'd reach the equivalent of Korea first, and then on to China. Based on the reduced scale, I didn't think the journey would take too long. Or I could turn around and cross the Pacific to the shrouded folk's equivalent of North America.

Where was Olivia most likely to be? They'd have taken her from our commune in the U.S., but there was no reason to assume they'd have kept her near there. They might have thought it wiser to bring her far away from the spot I'd be most inclined to look for her.

I rubbed my mouth in thought, and two of the shrouded folk glided into my line of sight. They slipped into the city farther down. Something about their course gave me the impression they had a definite destination in mind.

It was worth discovering what they found interesting in these macabre replicas of the human world. Setting my feet carefully, I crept over to follow them.

The dissonant sounds heightened slightly, niggling at my skin. A hint of color seeped across the buildings around me. I took a turn at an intersection and peered around a skyscraper after the shrouded ones. A ruddy glow emanated from up ahead. They were heading straight toward it.

I ventured down a side street to keep some distance,

the glow expanding with each block I passed. When I reached the skeletal park by what would have been Shinjuku station, I stopped and simply stared.

Where the immense train station would have been in my reality, a large spear of stone jutted toward the sky. It was shorter than many of the skyscrapers, which was why I hadn't seen it until I'd gotten closer, but at least a couple feet taller than I was. Its edges were a mix of jagged protrusions and misshapen lumps, as discordant as the warbling in the air. The warbling which had gotten even louder closer to the stone.

The sound seemed to echo a flickering red light that jerked and flared within the stone like flames whipped by the wind. Just looking at it made my stomach churn.

The shrouded folk clearly found the sight much more appealing. The two I'd been following drifted up to the stone and leaned toward it. They appeared to press the dark hollows of their faces directly to the surface of the rocky spear. Where they touched it, the crimson glow quaked.

They were absorbing some sort of energy from the stone, I concluded after watching for a few minutes. A hot, fiery energy... like the kind Earth's sun provided?

If this was what they fed on, no wonder they were so eager to cross over to the human world. Simply basking in our sun must be a hundred times more satisfying than what they could suck from one of those stones.

The shrouded folk lingered by the stone for a while longer. When they meandered off, they looked much more aimless. What did they fill their time with when they weren't drinking rocky glows or slipping into our world to prey on human beings?

I wasn't here to play anthropologist to the fiends. I was curious about this stone, though. I edged across the plaza and approached the spear.

The energy rippling off it jittered through my nerves even more forcefully. I had to grit my teeth to stop them from chattering. When I reached my hand toward the stone's surface, my stomach flipped so forcefully I nearly vomited. A wave of exhaustion washed over me.

Okay, that thing obviously wasn't going to do *me* any good. I backed up in a hurry, nearly stumbling over a low-rise.

As soon as I'd put several blocks between me and the glowing stone, the discordant energy began to fade again. My stomach settled and more of my energy returned. I dragged in a breath and considered what I'd learned.

The shrouded folk took power from those stones. In at least this case, the stone had been in the center of a major city. I hadn't seen any similar spears of rock jutting in the middle of the open plains, so maybe they were tied to the cities via whatever connection this realm had to mine.

The highest shrouded folk, the type who'd have captured my sister and been able to keep her prisoner all this time without any of the others making a sacrifice of her, would want to remain close to their power source, wouldn't they? Maybe there were different stones with different types or amounts of energy. They'd want to feed from the best.

I'd explore a few more cities and see what they offered, and then I'd be able to make a more educated guess at where Olivia might be held.

After a lot of walking, during which the sky never shifted in shade or brightness, I determined that every city that appeared in the shrouded realm did have a glowing stone, that all those stones glowed red, and that the ones in my vicinity all appeared to have about the same vibrancy. But as I ventured into the territory that mimicked mainland Asia, the crimson light began to spread beyond the stones. A faint line of it streaked along the plain I was crossing perhaps a quarter of a mile to my right. Not long after I'd spotted it, the erratic vibrations in the air had increased their effect.

I wasn't sure what the line was leading to, but it appeared to indicate more power. So I'd follow in the same direction as long as I could.

Unfortunately, the rising twitches of energy and warbles of sound were wearing at my own energy. My legs ached from the walking, and a tight pinch of tension had formed in the middle of my chest. That which fed the shrouded folk seemed to feed in turn on me. I supposed that wasn't much of a surprise.

I'd just have to hope I could find Olivia before this place wore me down completely.

The streak along the ground gleamed brighter as it reached a nearby city that I couldn't recognize on sight. I veered over to welcome the shelter of the buildings, even if the effects of that wavery red light would sap me even more. It was a trade-off. I'd passed a couple of shrouded folk at a distance out in the open now, and neither of them had accosted me, but from far away in my white sheet, I might have looked like one of their own. I had no idea how much the folk relied on sight.

Not long after I'd ventured into the city, wandering through its shrunken streets somewhat at random, a different sort of sound reached my ears—equally unnerving, but more purposeful. It was the tones of the shrouded folk's native language.

I crept around a cluster of high-rises and spied a few of the fiends in a sort of huddle not far from this city's glowing stone. The red light gave their streaming coverings a shifting pinkish tint like blood drifting in water.

The four of them were obviously discussing something without much concern of being overheard. The jerky, guttural sounds of the shrouded tongue didn't translate easily into language I knew, though—and when they were around humans, they usually spoke in words we'd understand.

During my time in the cult, I had learned to recognize a few of the sound combinations, the ones they used most frequently when talking about us. Now, I strained my ears, listening for anything familiar.

One of them said the word for human, and my heart skipped a beat. Were they talking about their communes across the realms… or about a human who might be trapped here?

Another repeated the word and said something about light or power—I could never quite distinguish between the two concepts in the way they spoke about them. They might be leeching some sort of power from Olivia the same way they did from the people in the cult. Would the rituals work with even more potency right here in the shrouded realm?

The conversation rambled in another direction I couldn't follow. Then the four fiends went abruptly silent. One of them said something with the word for "human" again. And they turned their fathomless faces in my direction.

I ducked down behind the building I'd been peeking around with a stutter of my pulse. I couldn't hope that they'd mistake me for a fellow monster up close. However they'd sensed me, I wasn't going to wait around to chat.

"Who is there?" one of the folk called out. Instead of answering, I darted down the street and around a corner as quickly and quietly as I could. I turned right and then left, hoping the weaving route would throw them off if they followed.

After a few minutes, I sank down in a courtyard between a circle of skyscrapers and listened. The warbling breeze quavered around me. I might have caught a far-off voice of a shrouded one in its own tongue. Nothing sounded nearby... but then, the folk didn't tend to make a lot of noise moving around.

Even if they'd given up searching, they'd be more on their guard now. They might pass on word to the other shrouded folk to keep watch for an unusual figure who could be human.

And I still wasn't sure I was even heading toward Olivia rather than away.

Shit.

I pressed the heels of my hands to my forehead and dragged in a slow breath. A sudden pang of longing filled my chest—to have Bash standing by, guns at the ready, whatever good they'd have done. Hell, to have Sherlock making his observations and leaps of deduction, John providing his buoyant optimism, Garrett full of fiery determination. To know I wasn't standing alone.

But I was. In the end, this was my fight, and I'd taken the necessary steps to keep it that way. I would *not* be so weak as to wish I'd brought those weaker than me into the fray.

Jemma Moriarty needed no one. That was how it'd always been, and how it had to be now if I wanted to make it through this realm alive.

*John*

As we strode to the hotel lifts, I bit my tongue just shy of asking Sherlock for the hundredth time if he was sure this was a good idea. At this point, determined as he was to get answers, I doubted "good" entered the equation.

I couldn't manage to stay totally quiet, though.

"What could she be doing here?" I said while we waited for a lift to arrive. "The cult wouldn't have a commune in the middle of a city, let alone one as big as Tokyo. And why would she need three whole floors to herself? It doesn't match her actions before at all."

"Which is exactly why we must discover what has changed and how that factor has altered her plans." Sherlock cast his sharp gaze over the lobby around us, unable to rein in his keen observational senses even when he believed our target was already in reach. "As for the hotel, she must have wanted a complete lack of distraction. We can assume the room she's using will be the middle of the three, with a buffer above and below, and that she'll have taken one at a distance from the lifts."

The sleek steel door opened with a chime. We got on alone. "Will we even be able to get access to those floors?" I started. "If she's taking measures that extreme…"

Sherlock brandished a plastic card he'd produced from his pocket. "I took the liberty of helping myself to a security key during our talk with the manager. That should get us all the access we need." He slid it into the opening beneath the control panel and pushed the button for the floor. The lift thrummed upward without hesitation.

Only Sherlock could have surreptitiously lifted a key card with his good arm broken. I'd be surprised if he hadn't specifically practiced that or similar maneuvers with his weaker side to prepare for this exact possibility.

Sherlock prepared for *every* possibility… until he couldn't. There was no way he could have anticipated the shrouded folk and their tactics. That didn't stop him from beating himself up for being taken off-guard, of course.

I glanced at him, searching for signs of the self-blame he'd expressed when we'd re-visited the mountain, but at the moment his pale eyes were bright with enthusiasm. There was very little the man liked more than being on the verge of solving a mystery, after all.

Before I could find myself gazing at my friend's distinctive face a little longer than was strictly *friendly*, my phone pinged with a text alert. I fished it out as the lift started to slow.

"Garrett wants to know if we got the right place," I reported. The detective inspector had unwillingly stayed behind in London after we'd finished the electronic side of our investigation. He'd already tried his chief's patience at

Scotland Yard with the other schemes of Jemma's we'd gotten caught up in, and now his expertise on the cult was in demand as other law enforcement agencies worldwide began to investigate.

"One day perhaps he'll develop more patience," Sherlock said, but he sounded only amused.

*We haven't determined yet,* I wrote back. *Will update you as I'm able.*

The hall the lift let us out into was completely silent. Glancing in either direction, I couldn't see the slightest hint of which door Jemma might be behind. My companion took a similar evaluation and set off to the left at a brisk stride, only a tad stiff with the battering he was still recovering from. I followed with a soft tap of my walking stick against the carpet.

Sherlock paused at the end of the hall and peered down at the carpet in front of the doors on either side. With a satisfied hum, he slid his keycard into the lock of the first door. I guessed it made sense not to give the inhabitants a chance to make a run for it, although it wasn't as if there was anywhere much they could run to this high up.

The lock clicked over, Sherlock nudged open the door —and a familiar brawny form charged into view, gun in hand.

Moran halted halfway down the suite's front hallway, staring at us, his normally impassive expression turned almost wild. His gun hand lowered but didn't drop all the way to his side. He looked over his shoulder and then back at us, his jaw working as he must have considered his options. Then he stepped toward us with a motion toward the hall that seemed to indicate he'd speak to us out there.

His silent urgency infected me. I kept quiet as he

joined us in the hall, and Sherlock held his tongue too. The second the door had closed, though, my friend spoke up.

"It's mainly Jemma we wanted to speak to."

"You can't," her associate said. "She isn't here."

Sherlock gave him a skeptical look. "I could lay out all the reasons I know that's a lie, or you could let us in without the bother. I'd rather not have to force the matter."

Moran let out an incredulous sound, his gaze falling to Sherlock's cast. He shook his head. "She obviously didn't push you hard enough," he said, but his tone was so wry that I didn't bristle at the remark.

"For her ends, perhaps not, although I'm quite glad she didn't err on the other side of caution. Are you letting us in or not?"

The other man grimaced. "It's... not as simple as all that. We're better off talking out here. She *isn't* exactly in the room. She's done a ritual so she can cross over to the place where her monsters live, and I'd rather not risk disturbing her. I don't know exactly what effects a disruption might have."

His silence and the floors of rooms booked made a sudden but unsettling sort of sense. "She's gone into the place the shrouded folk come from?" I said, a shiver running down my back. I'd only had limited dealings with the creatures myself, but I'd seen plenty of what they incited their worshippers to do to themselves and others, many of those victims children. Monster was the word for them, all right. "Why on earth would she do that? We were making so much progress cutting them off from this world."

Sherlock's forehead had furrowed. "They have something that's important to her."

"You could say that." Moran eyed us for a time, presumably debating the pros and cons of telling us more. The fact that Sherlock had arrived here at all must have made a pretty convincing case that simply telling us to get the hell out wasn't going to cut it.

He'd trusted us enough to reach out to us on Jemma's behalf once. I hoped we'd continued to justify that good will in the weeks since then.

Finally, he sighed. "I don't know how much she's told either of you about this, but growing up in her commune, she had a younger sister. When she escaped, she meant to come back and get her sister out too as soon as she had the resources. The monsters don't usually gobble up the kids until they're fifteen. She managed to get back there more than a year early, and her sister was gone, taken by them—dead, Jemma had to assume. But last week, one of the things came to her with proof that her sister is still alive, that they kept her rather than swallowing her up."

My stomach clenched. I remembered Jemma mentioning that the creatures had killed her sister—once, briefly—but I'd never pressed the subject. She'd also told me once when we were first getting to know each other that she'd lost someone she cared about a lot, and that was why she'd taken up the line of work she had. It wasn't hard to see how the grief and fury over the loss could have shaped her into a woman willing to do anything to destroy those monsters' influence over our world.

"Why would they tell her that now?" I asked, my voice rough.

Sherlock gave a humorless bark of a laugh. "To manipulate her into giving up her campaign, I'd imagine.

She was rooting them out, and they knew she might win that war. So they brought to bear the best card they had." He met Moran's gaze intently. "Do you think she has a chance of getting the girl out?"

"I have no idea," Moran said, and with those four words, I glimpsed the helplessness he must feel right now. "I'm not even clear on what the rescue is going to entail. I don't think she was either. She'd never traveled to their realm before—she had no idea what to expect."

"But she wanted us out of the way."

The hitman's mouth set in a grim line. "She was afraid you'd interfere in ways that would make the rescue harder for her. You *haven't* always been all that accepting of the supernatural ideas she's tried to explain to you."

That was a fair point, as Sherlock's grimace suggested he knew. He skipped addressing that point and moved on to the matter at hand. "She might need our help in this fiendish place, then?"

"I don't know how much we'd be able to do for her," Moran said, but I could hear the effort he was putting into that restraint. This wasn't a man used to sitting back and letting others do all the work.

"And you know how she arranged her passage into this realm? In theory, one or more of us could follow her there?"

"Someone needs to watch over her."

Sherlock crossed his arms over his chest, rather awkwardly with the one in its cast. "There are three of us. I'm sure that can be arranged."

Moran glanced toward the door. "We may not have enough supplies, either. There's a sort of salve she made that she smeared all over herself, and I don't think there's enough to cover another person as well as leaving extra if she needs it reapplied—and I couldn't tell you the exact proportions she used if we wanted to make more."

"I'm certain I could sort that out with a little investigation." Sherlock tipped his head toward the door. "Will you let us have a look? You should know by now we understand discretion."

Moran hesitated, but I suspected he'd already been mostly convinced. "She's in the living room. Be as quiet as possible. If we need to discuss anything, we can do that in the bedroom."

Sherlock and I nodded, and Moran eased open the door.

The air we stepped into was chilly enough to make me wish I'd brought a thicker shirt. A tart herbal smell hung in the air, lavender and feverfew and other scents Sherlock's well-trained nose would no doubt be able to pick apart. We snuck down the hall and came into view of the body lying still on the living room rug.

Flecks of those herbs stood out against Jemma's pale skin with a waxy shine. Her bright red hair was darkened by the same stuff, slicked close to her head. As I watched, one slow breath raised her chest and slipped away.

My medical instincts clanged with alarm. I had to clamp down on the urge to run to her and begin CPR. Nothing about her state looked healthy... but she understood what she'd done here better than I could hope to.

If I rushed in and ruined her attempt to save her sister, then I'd have proven her right for trying to keep us out of this scheme.

Sherlock walked close to her body with an air of scientific examination and then followed Moran into the kitchen. The hitman took out a bowl full of the herbal mixture and pointed to a box of supplies. Sherlock gave the stuff a stir and several sniffs, rubbed it between his fingers, and riffled through the box with minimal rustling. When he was finished, satisfaction practically radiated off him. He gestured for us to join him in the bedroom.

The TV was showing some historical drama—Hamlet, I gathered after a moment. Moran switched it off with the remote and no explanation. "Well?" he said to Sherlock.

"I believe I can recreate the mixture in the correct proportions," Sherlock said. "One of us would need to grab a few supplies, but nothing it should be difficult to find in Tokyo. White sheets should be simple enough as well. Are there any other necessary materials?"

Moran's hand went to his pocket. "I have sedatives she had me pick up. She took one right before she went into that state. I think the idea is to bring the body as close to death as it can get." His mouth twisted at saying those words aloud. "The only other aspect she mentioned is that once she was prepared and in position, she was going to focus on her interactions with the shrouded folk. I guess that helps her bridge the gap between those worlds."

"Not particularly scientific, but it serves as guidance enough. What sort of monitoring has she required since going into that state?"

"I haven't needed to do anything at all," Moran admitted. "She said if the salve absorbed into her skin, to apply more, but otherwise to leave her to it."

"It seems simple enough, then," Sherlock said. "Two of us will go after her to assist as well as we're able, and one will stay behind to ensure we don't cross all the way into death or otherwise meet an unfortunate end. I believe I should make the trip. My skills will serve her better in this other realm than waiting around here making the most simple observations."

Of course he'd see it that way. With the memory of Jemma's unearthly still body fresh in my mind, every part of me balked at the idea of seeing Sherlock enter the same state. But honestly, I knew I didn't have a hope in hell of talking him out of it.

Moran met my gaze when I glanced at him. The question came down to the two of us. My throat tightened with the desire to say I should be the one to join Sherlock—I was meant to stand beside him through every challenge any villain threw at us. And I wasn't entirely sure Jemma was done playing villain with him anymore than the shrouded folk were.

This mission wasn't about Sherlock, though. It was about Jemma. And I could read how desperately Bash wanted to come to her defense in the tension etched on his face, in every flex of his muscles.

He'd devoted years of his life to her. I'd never seen anything but total loyalty in him. He was meant for this.

If her judgment became questionable again, he had the best chance to making her see reason out of any of us.

I forced the admission out. "It makes the most sense for me to stay behind. I have the medical training. I'd be most likely to notice if any of you take a turn in a bad direction—and the most likely to be able to help you survive that. I can keep Garrett updated as well." I caught Moran's eyes again. "You ought to be able to go after her."

"Thank you," he said, his voice a little hoarse. He might not have expected that generosity from any of us. He turned to Sherlock. "Let me know what you need and if there's anywhere you think I can quickly find it, and I'll pick it up. I've got a driver on call."

Sherlock rattled off a brief list Moran entered into his phone. As the hitman left the bedroom, I caught Sherlock's good arm before he could follow.

"Can we talk for a minute?" I said. "You can't start preparing until he's back anyway, can you?"

"No," my friend acknowledged. He considered me with those cool eyes that missed so little. "You'd rather I didn't go."

"I just…" I made a face at the dresser. "You've been through two major health crises in the last couple weeks. Your body isn't completely recovered. We can't know exactly what effects the herbs and the drug and the rest will have on you. It's a greater risk than Jemma or Moran doing it."

*I've already nearly lost you twice. I don't want to have to face that again.*

"I've suffered no internal damage," Sherlock pointed out. "I can adjust the dosage if it seems wise—and you'll be here if anything begins to go wrong."

"I'd rather not have it get to that point," I muttered.

Sherlock fixed me with that calm gaze that could be so reassuring and yet also so frustrating. "This is the life I lead, John. The life you asked to be a part of. We go up against murderers and assassins. Danger is always lurking. What we do here could decide the security of the entire human race. You must see that I can't back down from that."

"I do," I said. "That doesn't mean I have to like it."

"I won't ask you to like it then." He gave me a sly little smile that woke up a completely different emotion in me.

This impulse I didn't rein in. I stepped closer to him, my hand rising to his shoulder, bobbing up on my toes slightly so I could bring my mouth flush against his.

Sherlock tensed just for an instant, but then he leaned into the kiss, his fingers coming to rest against my cheek, the warmth of his body flooding me.

God, I wanted so much more than this. The memory of our last bedroom encounter with Jemma, when Sherlock had stroked me to my release, tingled through me. But this was hardly the time or the place, and I'd only make him uncomfortable if I pushed for anything more.

I'd be honest with him, though. When we drew apart, his cheeks had turned pink in the most adorable way, as adorable as a man like Sherlock could be. "To clear our heads?" he suggested in a mildly teasing voice. It was the excuse he'd used, the excuse I'd used in turn, to justify little moments of intimacy in the past.

"No," I said. "Because I wanted to. Because I want you to know how much it matters to me that you come out of that monstrous place alive."

He didn't appear to know quite what to say to that. His gaze slipped away from mine for a second before returning. "I have every intention of returning," he said, which I knew was as close to a promise as he could give me.

# CHAPTER SIX

*Jemma*

I didn't see another significant change in the landscape of the shrouded realm until I reached a city I determined was Tehran from a couple of distinctive buildings and its relative position. The glowing red line I'd been following at a distance streaked straight into the middle of the city. I crept along the outskirts where the buildings would hide me but I wouldn't be venturing too close to this place's stone and its unsettling energy—or the shrouded folk who'd be feeding from it.

The farther I'd traveled along the line of light, the more persistent the erratic hum and crackle in the air had gotten. It itched at my skin and wobbled through my nerves. I hadn't felt any need to sleep or eat since I'd arrived here, other than the occasional pang of longing for a sugar cube to soothe my nerves, but my lungs were starting to clench around my breaths.

How much could I physically falter when my real physical form was back in the Tokyo hotel room? The body I had here might look a bit filmy, but it felt solid enough when I rubbed my arms.

Halfway around the city's edge, I came across another glowing line. The one I'd been following before veered east across the continent. This one, if my impressions were accurate, shimmered into the distance mostly to the south. If I followed that one, I suspected I'd end up in Africa.

I studied it for a while, debating whether to follow the new one and see where it led me or continue along the path I'd already been on. Unless that first path ended here? I slipped through the buildings to check, and no, the eastern line stretched onward toward the next shrunken cities.

Another thought tickled through my head. I continued around the border of the city until I came to a fourth line, this one heading north.

Hmm. So I had one line of escalating power moving to the east, and another line now bisecting it. I'd bet the two met in the middle where the stone of power stood. None of the other cities I'd passed had held two lines. What was special about this one?

I'd probably have to do a whole lot more walking to figure that out, and the wobbliness of the constant dissonant sounds was seeping into the muscles of my legs. I didn't even know if the mystery would do anything to help me find Olivia. Fuck. Maybe I should have started this journey from Scotland where the shrouded one had approached me with its warning in the first place.

I ventured toward the middle of the city to at least confirm my suspicion about the crossing of the lines. It wasn't hard to find this city's stone. The glow emanated even farther than the others had, prickling into me. This one was taller too. I stopped in the shelter of a crumbling building to study it at a distance.

The lines definitely crossed there. And that stone, maybe because of its starker glow and its size, was particularly popular with the shrouded folk. As I watched, at least a dozen drifted up to it to press their "faces" to the quavering crimson light.

None of them came along the north-south line, though. They mostly glided in from the west, some of them heading back the way they'd come, and some heading on farther east after they'd fed. That behavior suggested that if there were anything more interesting to discover, it probably lay along that line. So what was the other for?

I picked my way back through the streets, mulling over the possibilities and doing my best to ignore the shivers now running through my legs. I'd just reached the outskirts of the city when two pale forms snapped into being a few hundred feet away on the desolate plain beyond.

My first instinct was to bolt deeper into the city again. Before my legs had even started moving, though, I registered the position and details of the figures. They were lying sprawled on their backs—I hadn't seen any shrouded folk do that. And rather than faces of shadow wrapped in thin swaths of material, they had actual heads. Human heads.

Cult members—two of them joining in the ritual at the same time? I'd never seen that done before, but that didn't mean it couldn't happen. I had no interest in running into members of any commune either, even if they were less dangerous than the fiends.

I took a step backward, meaning to crouch behind a

nearby apartment block to watch, and both of the figures tentatively sat up. At the sight of their movements and a fall of all-too-familiar messy dark curls, my heart lurched. I hurried forward instead, glancing around quickly to make sure no shrouded folk had lingered nearby.

So many questions and so much emotion surged up through me as I reached the two men, but making sure they didn't die in their first five minutes in this realm had to be my first priority. I motioned for them to come meet me with a jerk of my arm, and as soon as they were close, I waved them on toward the city, hustling ahead of them and scanning the landscape. Of all the ridiculous stunts they could have pulled…

As soon as we'd reached the relative safety of the city outskirts, I spun on the two of them. "What the hell are you doing here?"

I aimed my glare at Bash, because it was easier to face him than Sherlock. And anyway, neither of them could have made it here if he hadn't allowed it to happen. He was the only one who'd known the ritual I'd gone through.

Both of them *looked* a little ridiculous wrapped in their sheets like bizarre togas. I supposed I looked pretty odd too. Bash tugged at one of the folds as he held my gaze, his mouth set at a pained angle.

"You know how persistent this one is. He and the doctor tracked us down. John's watching over us back in the hotel—you know he'll have a better eye for anything going physically wrong than I would have." He paused. "It's been almost a whole day since you passed through. There has to be *some* way we can help."

"You could have ended up anywhere! This realm is huge. You could have landed right in the middle of a bunch of shrouded folk, and that wouldn't have helped me at all."

"We adapted your use of mental focus," Sherlock said in his usual even voice. "As we went under, we trained our minds not just on the shrouded folk but on your presence. That strategy appears to have had the intended effect."

I let myself meet his eyes then. There was no recrimination in his expression, no sign that he was anything like angry… but then, Sherlock didn't generally give in to such base emotions, did he? My gaze dropped to his arms, the one of them held awkwardly in front of him in a cast that had made the trip with him, and my chest tightened.

"*You* should still be in a hospital."

One corner of his mouth quirked upward. "You should have killed me better if that was the outcome you were hoping for."

The fact that he could joke about what I'd done to him sent a clashing rush of fondness and guilt wrenching through me. Fondness, guilt, and fear.

I'd pushed him, meaning to push him right out of my life, so he couldn't inadvertently sabotage my attempt to rescue my sister, yes. But seeing him here sparked a totally different sort of horror. This was the most dangerous place any human being could be. I'd wanted to keep him—to keep all the men I cared about, as hard as I often found it to admit that affection—out of this.

"Moran told us about your sister," Sherlock added in a more serious tone. "I can understand, given the situation and the unexpected way it came upon you, why you might not have trusted any of us to approach it in the most constructive way."

"And yet here you are. You should hate me."

His smile came back. "You put more care into minimizing the actual harm in my supposed murder than most people put into their attempts at assisting those in need. Did you really think I wouldn't put the pieces together?"

"I thought the damned doctors would keep you in treatment long enough that it wouldn't matter," I muttered.

"Well, they didn't, and here I am to join the search. That seems the better outcome to me."

The outcome I'd been longing for hours ago. I choked up for a second despite my best efforts. It took me a moment before I was sure my voice would come out steady. "And now I might lose her *and* you. Did it never occur to you that I might rather have you alive and hating me than dead?"

Something in Sherlock's angular features softened. "Jemma, following other people's orders has never been a particular skill of mine. I invested in this 'case' of yours, and I invested in *you*, and if I have my way, I'll see it through to the end. I'm here now, so you may as well make use of me. In future, if you tell me to stay out, I won't follow. But you're not alone in this mission, and I needed you to know that, beyond any shadow of a doubt."

Future promises didn't do me much good now, but those last words brought back the lump in my throat. I didn't know what to say in response. Instead, I turned back to Bash.

"We're here at your service, Majesty," he said with a wry lilt to the nickname. "What have you found out so far? What are the next steps?"

I exhaled slowly. They *were* here now, and they might

be able to help, especially once I figured out where Olivia actually was. "If any of the shrouded folk come at you in an attack, you leave here immediately without waiting on me. Understood? All you have to do is pull the sheet up over your face to cover your eyes and focus on the room back home."

Sherlock nodded. Bash only grimaced. I gave him a stern look. "That's a direct order."

"If I can stop one of them from hurting you—"

I threw up my hands. "Fine! I'll just make sure it doesn't come to that. If my life isn't under threat but yours is, get the hell out of here. Now, let me tell you what I've determined about this place so far."

We walked the circuit of the city's edge, and I explained the way the shrouded realm appeared to mimic our world with its shrunken ruined replicas of the major human cities. I went on to touch on the stones with their unnerving energy, the line I'd been following and the new one that had appeared, and the behavior of the shrouded folk around them.

Sherlock peered intently at everything around us and broke my commentary only with an occasional question. When we came to the line that shone off to the south, he stopped and studied it for several minutes.

"From the observations you've related," he said, "I would predict that the primary line you've followed leads to some sort of central hub of greater power. Perhaps even one fueling the other stones via those lines. Which leads me to believe this secondary line may be a ring of some sort around what we might call the 'axle'."

As sharply observant as always. "I was thinking something similar," I said. "Given the distribution of cities across our world, I'd imagine that means there are likely other lines leading to that central point. The ring might connect them all the way around."

The detective rubbed his chin. "But we can't know how many or where they are without venturing along them. Where do you think these creatures would be most likely to hold your sister?"

"It's hard to know," I admitted. "I've never heard of the shrouded folk keeping a human sacrifice alive as a prisoner before, so I have no idea what might be necessary for that. My best guess was that they'd want to have her somewhere they had access to as much power as possible, but that is only a guess."

Bash shifted on his feet, gazing into the distance. "The space between the cities here is obviously a lot shorter than in the real world. I'm a big believer in getting the lay of the land before taking action. We could test out the theory about the ring and axle by following this line and seeing whether there are other 'spokes' in the cities it crosses through. If we don't have a better sense of where your sister is by the time we've explored that far, we could head on toward the center."

"Acquiring sufficient data to draw one's conclusions is a strategy I vastly prefer to any other," Sherlock said, with an approving dip of his head that left Bash a little startled looking. It was a good thing they were starting to get along, or their following me here would have been not just ridiculous but disastrous.

I brushed my hands together. "All right. That sounds reasonable. Let's get going then. I don't want to spend any longer in this realm than I have to."

I moved to talk forward, and my legs trembled under me at the sudden movement. Bash caught my arm before I stumbled. He examined my face, his own darkening with concern. "Are you all right? You haven't gotten hurt here, have you?"

I shook my head, making my best attempt at standing straight and steady. "It's the energies in this place. I'm sure they'll start to get to you too. They're constantly jarring my nerves—it's wearing me out. But I can keep going."

At least, I thought I could. I went to take another step, and my muscles wobbled again. My jaw clenched. I wouldn't be able to dodge the fiends very easily like this. I could end up being a liability to my men rather than the other way around.

"Have you found anything that counteracts the effects?" Sherlock asked.

I shook my head, fighting down my frustration. The discordant drone rattled on through my ears and into my body. My lungs constricted more tightly.

"Sit down for a moment?" Bash said, and I gave in to his suggestion. I let myself sink onto the pocked rooftop of a single-story building that only came up to my knees and dragged in a breath. Bash crouched beside me, his hand on my back. He rubbed it up and down over my spine in a ghost of a massage.

As the rhythm of the movement seeped into me, the jittering of my nerves started to fade. Even the erratic sounds themselves dulled around me. Interesting. I leaned into his touch encouragingly. "Something about *that* is helping."

Sherlock's eyes lit with inspiration. "Patterns, rhythms —anything repeated and predictable clashes with these creatures, doesn't it? It would make sense that the energy they thrive on would be repulsed the same way. Perhaps all you need is some rejuvenation time."

He sat at my other side and ran his hand over my

thigh, the warmth of his fingers grazing my skin through the thin fabric of the sheet. As he stroked them down to my knee and up again, Bash continued his light massage on my back. The unsettling dissonance drew back a little more. And a totally different sensation unfurled low in my belly.

Sherlock must have detected the shift in my mood before I'd even said anything. He added a swivel of his thumb and said in an overly offhand way, "Do you suppose a more intensive physical interaction might result in a swifter recovery, Miss Moriarty?"

What a Sherlockian approach to a proposition that was. I had to restrain a chuckle, but at the same time desire flared higher inside me.

"It might. I can't see how it'd hurt to experiment. What did you have in mind, Mr. Holmes?"

He glanced at Bash as if to confirm he wasn't walking into a minefield. My hitman rested his other hand on my waist. His stance beside me tensed for a second and then relaxed. He'd gradually gotten used to the idea that I enjoyed intimacy with the trio as much as I did with him —he'd even collaborated with Garrett to satisfy me in rather spectacular fashion a couple weeks ago. Add in the element of curing me of my ills, and he'd have even less reason to hesitate.

"I think I get the general idea," he said in a low voice, and drew his hand up to cup my breast.

It was hard to say what burned away the quivers that'd been setting me off balance more—the spark of pleasure at the swipe of his thumb over my already stiffening nipple or the rhythmic intensity with which he repeated the gesture. An approving hum crept up my throat. At the same time, Sherlock shifted his touch higher to tease his fingers over my sex.

I just about growled with need when he caressed my clit, sending pulses of heat through me with each swivel of his hand. The energy of the shrouded realm dwindled to a faint drone. I gripped Bash's shoulder, Sherlock's arm, my lips flushed with the longing to collide with theirs, but I hadn't lost my head so much I'd forgotten where we were and what dangers lurked here.

Intense was good, yes, but we couldn't lose ourselves in the moment here. If I was going to give myself over to these sensations, we'd better make sure no fiends spotted us while we were temporarily… distracted.

Bash moved his attentions to my other breast, and my head started to roll back of its own accord. My wandering gaze caught on a high-rise a short distance away that was big enough to cover what would have been an entire city block in the real world. Here that made it large enough to easily hold all three of us—and one side had a hole gouged in it nearly as tall as I was.

"I think we could use a little more privacy," I said, my voice coming out breathless, and tugged the guys upward. Sherlock spotted my intended destination in an instant. We made our way over to it as if as one being, their fingertips still gliding over my body tracing patterns of heat, my legs already stronger beneath me.

The building we ducked into had been nearly completely hollowed out, only the ridges of crumpled floors marking each story. Tiny streaks of light flowed through the windows. The shrouded folk stench filled my nose for a second. Sherlock had ended up in front of me. I yanked him to me, claiming his mouth and drowning myself in the mingled scents of tobacco and astringent aftershave that I was coming to adore.

From behind me, Bash pulled the sheet wrapped around me up, gathering it by my waist. A trace of the gel-like substance remained on my skin beneath it. He slicked it over my clit as Sherlock kissed me back hard, and I moaned into the other man's mouth.

The bulge of my right-hand man's erection brushed my ass, and a sharper longing rose up inside me. I tore my lips from Sherlock's just long enough to say, "I want you both inside me. As soon as possible."

Sherlock blinked in apparent confusion, but he wouldn't need much guidance for his part. I tugged at his sheet to free his cock, and he claimed my mouth again.

Bash understood what I'd meant. He slid his hand around my hip to probe my back entrance. I might have whined, just a little, as his finger traced that ring of muscle.

The two of them were too damn tall. I gripped Sherlock's shoulders, he clasped my thigh with his good hand, and Bash steadied me from behind. With a heft, the detective had positioned me over his cock. I arched toward him, dropping my hips, and he sheathed himself inside me with a single giddying thrust.

It wasn't quite enough, but Bash was ready. He dipped his slick fingers inside me and ran them around my other opening in a blissful rhythm until I let out an impatient sound to get on with it. The head of his cock brushed my ass and slowly penetrated me with his perfect control and the most delicious burn.

Sherlock's eyes had widened. In his limited experience, this kind of joint intimacy might never have occurred to him. I kissed him through a gasp of pleasure, and any inhibitions that might have woken in him fell away. With a groan, he started to rock in and out of me.

Bash matched his pace from behind. Both of them filled me and nearly released me together, over and over. The pleasure of it thrummed through every inch of my being, chasing any last tremors of the shrouded realm's energy away.

"Jemma," Sherlock murmured, with a raw joy that shot straight to my heart. I clutched him and reached my other hand back to caress Bash behind me. The rush of bliss careened through me faster than ever before. I choked back a cry, and my body shuddered between them as I came so hard my vision dissolved into a burst of light.

Bash let out a strained sound at the clench of my muscles. He pressed his mouth to the back of my neck as he followed me. Sherlock's breath broke. He pumped into me faster, and then he was flooding me with the heat of his own release.

My body slumped between them, tingling and sated, held by these two very different men who'd traveled across unimaginable distances to stand with me. For the first time in hours, I felt fully like myself again.

"Rejuvenation complete," I said with a smirk, and Bash chuckled against my skin. "Let's see what other surprises this realm has in store for us."

# CHAPTER SEVEN

*Garrett*

Even if I hated being sidelined from Sherlock's investigations abroad, I had to enjoy the irony of my current situation. Just weeks ago, the chief had been hassling me about focusing too much on the cases involving the shrouded folk's cult. Now that a second commune had been revealed and raided within the UK, and with countries all across the world starting to take notice, I'd been given a small office of my own here at the Yard specifically to coordinate with the rest of an international task force dedicated to uncovering the extent of this toxic presence in our midst.

Since I was the only one on that task force who'd had direct dealing with multiple communes, an awful lot of the coordination fell on my shoulders.

"That's right," I said to the sergeant from Rome who'd started aiding investigations into the nearby hill country. "The most common signs are periodic thefts of medical supplies, food, and other essentials. You'll also want to watch for reports of any unusual violent activity—mutilated animals, destruction of property—and a higher number of missing persons than in the surrounding areas. The communes tend to choose areas at or near high elevations, often forested so they can avoid their buildings being spotted from above."

"It was a thing like that that made me concerned to start with," the sergeant said in lightly stilted English. With some of my law enforcement brethren across the world, we'd needed to rely on translators. "I can look for these other signs."

If he'd seen enough to reach out, chances were high that we had a real case there. I jotted a couple notes on my notepad. "Proceed with caution if you see more indications that you have an active commune in the area. They may be on higher alert now that we've started cracking down elsewhere. We want to bring these people in, not have them run off to start up all over again someplace else."

"Agreed." The sergeant's tone turned solemn. "I've read some of the reports, seen the pictures… We want people like that locked away."

After hanging up, I added his details to my quickly growing computer database. In just the three days since I'd returned to Scotland Yard while Sherlock and John determined Jemma's likely location and then followed her, the task force had already identified five likely commune locations in the United States, Spain, Norway, Morocco, and Peru, with dozens more suspected across the globe. If we could prove as effective at shutting down those communes as at finding them, the demonic beings egging on the cult wouldn't stand a chance.

Although from what John had relayed to me about

Jemma and her sister, that might not be enough for her to declare victory.

The conflicting emotions that rose up at the thought of Jemma—the brilliant, determined woman I'd fallen for… who also thought it totally reasonable to push a man down a mountain to achieve her goals—only had a moment to stew inside me before a knock sounded on my door. At my "Come in," Chief Higgins poked his head in.

"Lestrade," he said with a strange air, his usual unshakeable authority off-balance in the face of my new, prominent assignment. "There's been an incident in Southwark I think you might want to look into."

I frowned. "In *Southwark*?" The communes within our borders hadn't been anywhere near London. They hadn't been anywhere near any major habitation. The cultists wanted to be left alone, not draw notice.

He motioned to my computer. "I've forwarded the relevant materials. It's all over the news. A small group of civilians just gave The Shard a good battering with a couple of potent homemade bombs. There are certain details about their behavior that reminded me of your bizarro cult."

A chill ran over my skin. Why the hell would the shrouded folk's worshippers suddenly be bombing major urban buildings? That didn't fit their typical MO in any way I could see, though maybe Sherlock would have had an immediate answer.

"I'll take a look," I said. "Thank you."

He gave me a curt nod and strode away.

I pulled up the files with trepidation squeezing my gut. Maybe the chief was grasping at straws trying to find a connection to my new work focus so he could stay involved, or maybe he was being overly paranoid about the slightest hint of activity that reminded him of the cult reports out of worry he'd let something slip by on his watch. It could have nothing to do with them at all.

But usually Chief Higgins was pretty level-headed. That was why I'd generally appreciated working under him. If he thought this event might be related, it was worth digging into right away.

The first photos made me wince. The Shard was aptly named considering it looked like a perfectly constructed spire of glass rising above all the nearby buildings in Southwark. Whoever this group was, their homemade bombs had shattered some of the panes and blackened others from the base to nearly halfway up the building. The effect gave it a lopsided, ravaged sort of look that was the exact opposite of its normally crystalline—if a little outlandish—appearance.

Several workers had been taken to the hospital to have burns and other injuries treated, but it didn't appear the bombs had left any fatalities. The reports suggested that the perpetrators had been focused on damaging the outside of the building more than anyone inside it. That was certainly unusual.

Then I came to a portion that described the men and women taken into custody. The officers had encountered them still in the building, "swaying in strange motions and mumbling to themselves as they bled from cuts they appeared to have sliced into their own arms and legs."

My stomach flipped over. That sounded like our cultists, all right. Jemma had said the bloodletting was part of their worship—the shrouded folk enjoyed the pain. It definitely wasn't the sort of behavior you'd expect from any ordinary bombers. What the hell were they up to?

I read through the rest of the materials the chief had sent me and then headed right out the door. I wasn't going to find out much secondhand. The real answers would be on the scene. And damn if I didn't wish Sherlock were along to make his astute observations.

He and John had gone off to handle one side of things. This part of the case was mine. I hadn't been made detective inspector younger than anyone else on the force for nothing, and I'd better prove that.

The bombing had only happened a little more than an hour ago. When I reached The Shard, the streets around the building were cordoned off with police tape. I ducked under one of the yellow strips and flashed my badge at the constables who moved to intercept me.

"This crime may be related to a special investigation I'm working on," I said. "I need to see the site of the bombing and to talk to any of the perps who are available."

The one guy nodded. "We've got a couple waiting for transport. There were a bunch of them all coordinated. I'll show you what I can of the site, and then you can have at them."

The damage looked even more offensive up close, like a massive dappled scar running up the side of the building. The constable walked me over to the base, where the panes had been completely blasted away, and pointed upward to a charred hole in the edge of the first floor ceiling.

"They had two explosives that both packed a lot of punch considering they probably bought the stuff at a gardening store. One they set off on the second floor and the other on the tenth. We haven't confirmed possible structural damage yet, so everyone's been ordered to evacuate except the inspectors."

I wasn't going to get any closer then. The sunlight slanting through the gaping openings where glass should have been caught on a reddish glint at the edge of the hole. I squinted at it. "I heard the perps were cutting themselves?"

The constable made a face. "It's a real mess up there. Blood all over the floor. From the marks on them, it wasn't the first time they'd hacked into themselves like that. Bloody lunatics."

If these people were part of the cult, he didn't know the half of it. I poked around at the rubble on the ground, shards of glass clinking against each other, but no flashes of inspiration came to me. Making obscure connections wasn't how I'd gotten this job anyway.

"Let's see these people, then."

The two who hadn't been shipped off yet were sitting in the back of a police van that needed a driver. The woman, who looked to be in her mid-thirties, glanced up with a defiant expression as I came in. The man—older, maybe fifty—shifted farther back on the bench. They'd both been cuffed, and bandages covered most of their arms, calves, and even the back of the woman's shoulder.

"Give me a moment?" I said to the constable. He drew back to rejoin his colleague.

When we were alone, I turned to the two criminals. "So," I said, as if I already knew everything, "you worship *them*, do you?"

A flash of doubt crossed the woman's face. "What we do is none of your business," she spat at me.

"I think it is when you go around blasting holes in buildings in my city." I propped myself against the wall. "I know they like you bleeding and all that, but they don't usually encourage you to draw attention to yourselves. Trying out a new approach?"

"We serve as we're asked to serve," the man mumbled.

The woman shot him a glare. "I'm not saying anything to you," she informed me.

Nothing they'd said quite confirmed it, only they were part of some barmy collective. I took a small gamble. We'd only identified three areas of cult activity in the country, and two of those communes had been thoroughly raided. One group, however, had fled before we'd tracked them down. Chances were, if these were shrouded folk worshippers, they'd be that bunch, not some roaming from across the Channel or farther abroad.

"I don't need you to say anything." I tipped my head to the two of them. "Mostly I just wanted to see you. We know you came from that little settlement out by Dover. Nice trick burning all your things, but it didn't work quite as well as I'd imagine you wanted."

The man clearly wasn't as self-controlled as his companion. He swore under his breath, hunching defensively. The woman couldn't help reacting on a smaller level, her hands clenching in the cuffs. Her mouth tightened.

"You know *nothing*," she sneered, but she couldn't hide the nervousness in her expression.

"Oh, I think I've already proven that's not true. You could enlighten me on one point, though. Why The Shard? What's it ever done to your gods?"

The woman stared toward the little windows in the doors, and a little shudder ran through her. This time, though, her mouth stayed clamped shut.

I didn't think I was going to get anything else out of

these two right now. They'd given away enough. The rest I could follow up on with the rest of the group in custody —pick out the one who looked most likely to talk, get them alone, a little good-cop-bad-cop routine… It might take some time, but we'd get our answers.

If we had time.

I waved my thanks and good-bye to the other officers and headed back to my car. A cloud of uneasiness followed me. When I sank into the driver's seat, I reached for the key, hesitated, and got out my phone instead.

John picked up on the third ring. "No news here yet," he said, sounding even more tense than he had when I'd spoken to him first thing this morning. It had to be early in the morning over there in Japan now, but I didn't get the impression I'd woken him. Was he sleeping during the unearthly vigil he was keeping over there? I sure as hell didn't envy him his current job.

"I didn't figure there was," I said. "Because of course you'd tell me as soon as there is. I'm calling because *I* have news. It looks like the shrouded folk are encouraging their cult to take up a new MO."

John's voice turned more alert in an instant. "What's that?"

I peered at the scarred form of The Shard through my windshield. "You remember that commune you and Moran found abandoned and scorched? I think we've found its former inhabitants. They just blew up part of The Shard while swaying and bleeding all over it in worship."

"*What?* Why the hell—they're meant to keep themselves secret."

"They used to be meant to, anyway. One of the guys I talked to made it sound as if they were asked to do it. I don't suppose you've seen anything over there or heard anything from Moran that would give you a clue as to why."

There was a rustle as John must have shaken his head. "Not at all. That's the last thing I'd have expected. Bloody hell. They didn't give you any indication of their reasons?"

"Not really. I haven't had much chance to go at them yet. I wanted to check in with you first."

"You're worried," John said. Sherlock might have been the observational genius, but the former doctor didn't miss much when it came to emotions.

There was no point in denying it. "I'm just thinking, there are dozens, maybe hundreds of these little communes we haven't taken down yet. What if this isn't an isolated incident? What if it's part of some new backlash against our efforts and Jemma's?" *What if it happens again, and next time we lose more than part of a pretty building?*

"That... that doesn't seem like an unreasonable concern." John sucked in a breath. "As soon as Sherlock, Jemma, and Bash come out of that place, I'll see what they think. But you've got your task force in place. I'd imagine you can handle this more effectively than any of us could."

I could. I'd already been thinking through how I'd reach out to my contacts, make suggestions of activity to watch out for—in major cities, around visually striking buildings and other public places... This was the kind of work I was meant to do. I hadn't been totally prepared for John to recognize that, though.

Maybe that was unfair of me.

"If there's any way you think I can contribute, just let me know," John went on, and it hit me that I wasn't on

the sidelines this time, not really. I was in the middle of
the fray, calling the shots.

I'd spent so long feeling as if I was chasing along
behind Sherlock's coattails, envying his easy partnership
with John… but if the events of the last few months had
shown me anything, it was that a hell of a lot of the
bitterness I'd been holding onto was my own doing. I had
to stop getting in my own way and get on with things.

"I appreciate that," I said. "I'd better get back to the
Yard and start coordinating."

I *was* calling the shots—and I'd better make sure they
were the right ones, or Lord only knew what kind of
catastrophe the world was about to face.

# CHAPTER EIGHT

*Jemma*

"Another spoke in the wheel," Sherlock said with a triumphant air.

We studied our current shrunken city's glowing stone from a safe distance. Sherlock's natural pallor had taken on a yellowish cast in the hours we'd been hiking across the shrouded realm, but the sight of two lines of ruddy energy crossing at the stone brought a flush back into his cheeks. There wasn't much that invigorated him more than confirming one of his theories was correct.

I glanced around at the downtown buildings, like a crumbling toy city we'd barged into. I hadn't recognized this place as we'd come up on it, but Sherlock had immediately declared it Nairobi. We'd passed several other cities large enough to make an appearance in the shrouded realm on the way here, but the south-aiming line we'd been following had traveled through them and their stones without any intersection. I'd been starting to wonder if the detective might have been mistaken just this once.

"It could be more of a grid than a wheel," Bash remarked from behind me. He'd set his hand on my shoulder when we'd stopped, his thumb swiveling in a steady motion to push back the creeping shivers the erratic sounds around us brought on. *He* was feeling the effects too, as much as he tried to hide any shaky moments from me. I rested my hand over his to return the favor with the stroke of my fingers.

"Based on the trajectory through the cities, the line we've been tracking isn't straight but curved," I said. "At this point, I'm convinced." I turned my gaze toward the gleaming line that formed the spoke. "The real question is, what are we going to find at the center?"

I couldn't say I was looking forward to finding out. The dissonant energy of the shrouded realm had stayed at the same moderate level while we'd been navigating the ring. I suspected as soon as we headed closer to the center, it'd escalate again.

But I hadn't seen any trace of my sister or anything to suggest where Olivia might be in our travels so far. It appeared increasingly certain that the fiends would be holding her by the main source of their power. Not only would they be better equipped to control her, but the heightened energy would have sapped her strength away too. How had she even survived in this place for years when it was wearing me down after just a couple days?

The thought of all that time she'd remained a captive made me queasy. I squared my shoulders and raised my chin toward the path ahead of us. "Why don't we get going? If it takes us much longer to get back, John will worry himself frantic."

"True." Sherlock studied the pale-cloaked bodies of the shrouded folk drifting along the line of energy. "It appears we'll have more company heading in that direction. How would you suggest we avoid notice?"

"We won't walk right by the line. Better to keep a good distance, just close enough that we can still follow it. And we can adjust our sheets so they look more like the fiends' coverings." I tugged one of the folds by my back up over my head to hide my bright hair. "That also means you can escape back to our world faster if one of the creatures comes at you. Just be careful not to drop the fabric over your eyes accidentally."

We took a winding path back through the city so that we emerged a good stretch away from the line we meant to follow. It glimmered across the dull ground like a thread of flame. With the way the ring had curved, I calculated we were now heading more north than east. Up into northern Africa or even further, into Europe?

Did these crossroads have any impact on the real cities they were associated with? In my travels, I'd never noticed any urban areas that gave me an uneasy vibe, but then, I hadn't been looking for signs of shrouded folk presence amid the bustle.

Before we left the replica of Nairobi behind, Bash and Sherlock raised their sheets over their heads like I had. "The fiends have a certain way of moving that we can imitate to some extent too," I told them, and demonstrated the long, smooth strides I'd perfected while I'd been heading deeper into the creatures' territory rather than skirting it.

A dozen or so shrouded folk drifted right along the glowing line in our view. From our vantage point, they were little more than pale blobs in vaguely human form. We shouldn't look much different. When I'd traveled alone, none had come to investigate other than that bunch I'd gotten too close to early on.

Three of us making the journey together might have looked even less suspicious. Many of the fiends appeared to cluster into groups of anywhere from two to four as they made their way across the plain.

It was another long walk. Every time we passed a city, we kept to the fringes and watched for intersecting lines, but as before, the first several didn't offer anything new. The unnerving sounds constantly traveling through the realm started to ring in my ears. I felt a little childish doing it, but after a while I grasped both of the guys' hands while we walked, tracing patterns over their knuckles. They caught on and returned the gesture without any of us commenting on it. That strategy held off the discordant energy enough that my legs only twinged rather than aching.

Sherlock's eyes must have been a tad keener than my own. Before I'd noticed anything, he squinted at the next city up ahead and said, "I think we've found our axle."

I peered at the landscape around the miniature skyline as we drew closer. Within a minute, I spotted what he meant. Another glowing line to our right streaked across the plain toward that city, but at an angle sharper than ninety degrees. It could very well be the same line I'd followed into Tehran.

"That's Istanbul," I said, tipping my head toward the distinctive form of the Hagia Sophia. I'd spent a little time there for business reasons twice in the last several years— I'd found it a fascinating mix of ancient history and modern developments. The thought of the shrouded folk feeding off it even in some distant, detached way made my skin crawl.

"You haven't seen any real-world analogue for a power base there?" Sherlock asked, his hand warm and dry against mine.

I shook my head. "I never would have thought the shrouded folk interacted with our world in any significant way other than through the communes, and all of those I know about are nowhere near cities." But since I'd ramped up my campaign against the fiends, it'd become increasingly and uncomfortably clear how much I hadn't found out about them in my limited view as a child in one of those communes.

More shrouded folk were traveling toward the city along the second line. How many of those glowing trails came together in this city? We'd want to find out, but apprehension shivered through me alongside the rising erratic thrum. The place might be crawling with the fiends. We couldn't hope that we could fool them with distance once we got closer to the point where all those paths converged.

One could slip around unnoticed much more easily than three. I squeezed the guys' hands a little tighter as we reached the first of the buildings, the normal urban sprawl constricted to just the city proper as it had been in the other replicas we'd encountered. I might not have made it this far without Bash and Sherlock's support; it squeezed my heart thinking that they'd been willing to risk so much to try to help me. But the fact was that they were even more vulnerable here than I was, and I couldn't think of any way they could defend themselves, let alone me, if we got into a real altercation.

I noted a long apartment block up ahead, its ten stories looming only twice my height, and veered toward it. The entire eastern wall had caved in, leaving the interior strewn with rubble but open to intruders. I stopped in front of it and let go of the guys, ignoring the jolt of loss at the lack of contact.

"I'll scout out the city center on my own," I said in the most authoritarian tone I had in me. I fixed Bash and then Sherlock with a look imbued with the same steel. "I know you probably hate the sound of that plan, but it makes more sense than anything else we could do. I think you've done everything you can to get me through this place. We're *all* safer if we're not roaming around this city together. And I can avoid the fiends better than you two."

"Mori," Bash said, not quite a protest, with an uneasy twist of his mouth.

I gripped his arm. "I'll just take a quick look, see if I can find any sign of my sister, and then I'll come back and share my observations, and we can decide what to do next from there. I survived three years as a teenager with no real-world experience before I ever hired you. I can make it through an hour or two on my own here."

Sherlock didn't exactly look pleased, but I'd known an appeal to logic would work on him. "I would rather make my own observations. Two sets of eyes may notice more than one."

"And you can make those observations after I've taken the lay of the land," I said. "I can prepare you for the threats. Think of this just as an initial scouting mission."

He let out an impatient breath, but he stepped into the shelter of the ruined building. Bash followed him reluctantly a moment later.

"It'd better be only an hour or two," my hitman said. "If it's any longer, I'm not waiting around here."

"I'll be back," I promised. "And if the fiends stumble on you in here, remember how to get home. I'll follow you back as soon as I see you're gone."

The grimace he gave me in response didn't exactly reassure me that he'd stick to that agreement, but I could tell it was the best I was going to get.

I slunk away through the streets. We'd entered on the old town side, most of the buildings no taller than me if not shorter, but the modern skyscrapers I glimpsed over the crumbling rooftops didn't glint the way they did in my reality. Of course, there wasn't anything much like sunlight here to glint off them.

The dryly rotten stink of the shrouded folk hung so thick along the streets that within minutes it had coated the inside of my mouth. I resisted the urge to spit. At every intersection, I peered both ways before crossing, checking for a different sort of traffic. A couple of times, I caught sight of shrouded folk passing farther along in one direction or the other, and hung back until they'd drifted out of sight.

The red glow started to tint the streets up ahead as I hurried across the wider gap where rippling waters of the Golden Horn should have been. The ground rose only slightly where I remembered a steeper hill from my explorations in my own world. I passed a half-toppled Galata Tower, picking my way carefully and quietly over the fallen stones, and jerked close to the nearest building at the murmuring of fiendish voices nearby.

A clot of five or six of them passed within ten feet of me, their conversation just loud enough for me to hear, even if I couldn't understand most of it. I caught the word for *human* again, and a term that had something to do with heights. I didn't think that could be referring to my or the guys' presence here. Was my sister here—in one of the tall buildings, maybe?

As I crept after them, I scanned the structures around me for any sign of activity within or on the rooftops. Nothing stood out. The crimson light intensified, painting the street, the buildings, and the sheet that covered me.

A thicker mass of shrouded folk stood around the source of that light. I sidled carefully around the nearby structures until I found a spot where the roofs were low enough that I could see over them if I leveraged myself partway up with my foot in a smashed crevice.

The stone spear jutting up in the midst of the city was twice as tall as any I'd seen before, its light pulsing in a stuttered beat and flaring red-hot. Shrouded folk clustered all around the stone, brushing it not just with their faces but the rest of their bodies. Five glowing lines flowed into it at nearly equal intervals around the spot. A wheel with five spokes.

A tickle of curiosity ran through me at the question of what the other three ring cities might be, but it was quickly overwhelmed by frustration. I'd come all this way, I'd heard the fiends talking about a human, but there was no sign of Olivia or any kind of human prison here either. They could have meant humans from their cult or who knew what else.

I dragged in a breath and closed my eyes. She had to be *somewhere*. If I could just latch onto the slightest trace of her presence...

I drew memories up in my mind: her smiling face

when I'd made her little animals out of folded paper, the closest things to toys we'd had. The way she would clutch my hand when the other kids tried to harass her. Her voice, bright and sweet, in the rare moments when no one else could hear her and she'd been happy enough to sing.

The sensations from those moments flooded me. "Olivia," I whispered against the discordant thrum. "*Olivia.*"

And like a miracle, that bright voice, though faint and ragged, floated to my ears.

"Jemma?"

My eyes popped open. Nothing lay around me except the same scene I've been watching before. "Olivia," I said again, a touch louder, straining my eyes.

The outline of a form, pale-haired and pale-dressed and the size of a grown woman—swam into view a few feet away from me. It was so transparent I couldn't make out her features, couldn't look into her eyes, but I felt down to my bones it was my sister.

Only… not really here.

"You shouldn't be there," she said in a frightened tone, the words sounding as if they'd crossed a vast distance.

"I came for you," I said. "Where *are* you?"

"On the other side. They say I'm… I'm an anchor for their stone, a bridge for the power."

My heart sank. After everything I'd risked here… "You're still in the human world."

Her head bowed in acknowledgment. Then her body twitched. "You have to go. Now. Fast. I can feel them— they're coming for you."

Her form snapped away, and I found myself staring through the spot where it'd been toward the massive stone spear. The massive stone spear and the shrouded bodies around it, several of which had turned my way.

Shit.

If I'd been here alone, I'd have jerked my "shroud" down over my eyes and willed my way home. My sister had been back there all along anyway. But Bash and Sherlock were waiting for me, and the fiends wouldn't necessarily stop searching just because I vanished from sight.

I leapt off the building and ran back the way I'd come.

The warbles of unnerving energy blared even louder, as if they were chasing after me in a wave of sound. I dodged fallen rubble and dashed left and then right between the streets. A tremor ran up my legs. I pushed myself faster—and one calf gave, pitching me across the road.

Pain and blood welled on my knees. I shoved myself back onto my feet and ran on, grasping the corners of the shrunken buildings around me for extra support.

The hiss of those swaths of dead flesh mingled with the energy's hum. I swerved around another corner and caught sight of the building where the men had taken shelter up ahead.

At the same moment, a shrouded one flew into the street in front of me.

My legs stalled. Then I hurtled forward, slamming past it with all the strength and speed left in my body. The brush of its shrouded form against my skin left my stomach lurching.

"We've got to go back home!" I called out. "Get out of here now! She isn't here!"

Bash appeared in the opening. At the sight of me and my pursuers, he moved to lunge forward. "No!" I yelled, and did the only thing I could think of that would force him to follow my orders. Shoving down the flash of panic at the thought of leaving him and Sherlock behind, I yanked the white fabric over my eyes and threw my consciousness back to the Tokyo hotel room.

# CHAPTER NINE

*Jemma*

I jolted awake on the carpeted floor with a jerk of my limbs as if an electric shock had raced through them. For a few seconds, I could only stare at the high white ceiling as the haze cleared from my head. Midday sunlight washed over my face. The sour smell of the shrouded realm lingered in my mouth. My muscles felt like jelly, and a knot of hunger twisted my stomach.

How long had I been gone from this world? The hours had started to blur together on the other side.

There was the scrape of chair legs against the floor, and then John was kneeling over me, his face tight with concern. "Jemma! Can you understand me? Are you all right?"

A form next to me shuddered and gulped air with a rasp. I managed to sit up, gripping John's hand for balance. Bash was just coming to, his face gleaming with the same herbal mixture that was still smeared all over me. Beyond him, a tremor ran through Sherlock's prone body.

The detective's eyes popped open, and relief washed through me—followed by another spasm of hunger.

I opened my mouth to speak and found my throat was too dry to force any sound out. John hustled to the kitchenette. After a brief clatter of glass and hiss of the faucet, he returned clutching three cups of water. I snatched one out of his grasp and practically inhaled it.

The liquid soothed my throat but barely touched the pangs in my stomach. I set the empty glass down and wobbled onto my feet. "We should eat something," I said in a rasp. "Our bodies need to recover."

Thankfully, I'd considered that factor when we'd stocked up the suite. I grabbed the loaf of bread on the counter and started slathering it with peanut butter. Because I hadn't left my sweet tooth behind in the shrouded realm, I also drizzled it with a good portion of honey.

By the time I'd finished assembling the first sandwich, Bash had made his way over to me on legs that only swayed a little. I tried to shove the food toward him, but he shook his head emphatically. "You were over there a lot longer than us. You need it more than I do. I can make one for myself and for Sherlock."

I might have argued more if saliva hadn't been flooding my tongue and my entire abdomen clanging for relief. Dropping onto one of the kitchen stools, I shoved a good quarter of the sandwich into my mouth in one go. Oh, Lord, that was just about the best thing I'd ever eaten.

After the first bite, I forced myself to take smaller nibbles and chew slowly despite my bodily sense of urgency. John helped Sherlock over to the counter, somewhat to the detective's dismay from his expression, though he didn't fight the help. As Bash slid over a hastily prepared sandwich, I spoke up, a little more clearly this time.

"Don't take it down too fast. When you've gone a while without food, you can make yourself sick if you gorge yourself."

As I knew from personal experience. The cult's favorite methods of physical torment involved outer injuries, but my commune had experimented with various sorts of deprivation when the mood struck them.

Sherlock nodded, probably already aware of that fact, and dug into his sandwich with some restraint. John hovered beside him, his anxious gaze sliding from his friend to me and back again. With my knot of hunger unraveling, it sank in that he might be as much nervous *of* me as for me, especially when it came to the man beside him.

"Even though he showed up uninvited, I refrained from giving him another shove," I said, breaking the silence. "He isn't in any more danger from me."

John blinked at me, and I tensed with the suspicion that I'd been too flippant in my sort-of reassurance. After what I'd set him up to witness the other day, he didn't have any reason to believe me on my second point, did he?

Sherlock broke the momentary silence. "I don't believe I ever was," he said mildly, and popped the last bite of his sandwich into his mouth.

"Apparently not, considering you made it here." I glowered at him. "If you do die, it'll definitely be *your* fault for not taking the hint."

"I accept that fact without complaint."

As John watched the exchange, his expression gradually relaxed into a bemused smile. "You're both insane," he informed us. "It's a good thing you've got people on your side who are patient enough to put up with it."

Bash had recovered enough to grab us all fresh glasses of water. He set them on the counter with his eyebrows raised. "Can you imagine if the two of them were left to their own devices to work together unchecked? I'm not sure if the results would be astonishing or terrifying."

"Hey. A little loyalty?" I aimed a teasing kick at his leg, and he shot me a fond grin as he dodged it.

John shook his head at the three of us. I wasn't sure he was completely reassured, but at least I didn't feel any immediate animosity from him. My gaze slid around the room, and now that my most pressing physical needs had been met, the sense of someone missing sent a different sort of pang through me.

"Garrett opted not to join you?" I said tentatively. As much as John was wary of me, it'd mainly be on Sherlock's behalf. Garrett Lestrade had always been the most uneasy of the bunch about my criminal inclinations in general. He took the letter of the law more seriously than the independent detective pair. He'd come to terms with my past, accepted me and opened up to me, even told me he loved me... but that was before he'd had to watch me assault one of his closest colleagues.

I couldn't say I returned the same depth of feeling he'd offered me—I wasn't sure I was capable of it—but the thought that he might be repulsed by me now sent a jabbing sensation through my chest.

"Oh, he'd have been here if he could," John said. "Duty called back in London. But he's still on the case. He's playing a key role in a task force investigating the cult's communes worldwide." He paused, his smile falling away. "That reminds me. I talked to him early this morning—he had something disturbing to report. It looks like the commune down near Dover—the one that scattered before we could catch them—launched an attack on The Shard. They blasted a large portion of the external walls, along with all the bloodletting and so one that they usually do."

My spine stiffened. "They attacked a public building in the middle of the city?" That *was* disturbing. What the hell were they up to? "Were they caught?"

"As far as Garrett could tell, they didn't make much effort to avoid arrest. One of the cultists he spoke to gave the impression that the shrouded folk had asked them to do it."

I didn't like the sound of that at all. It was probably a reaction to our attempts to shut down the cult—and it was a major escalation.

Sherlock's eyes sharpened in thought. "These beings don't care for patterns or mathematics. The Shard is a particularly… geometric building. Would that be the reason for making it a target?"

"Most likely," I said. "If just having the cult damage themselves and each other gives the shrouded folk energy, then damaging something that large and distasteful to them probably brings a whole lot more. They just wouldn't have done it before because sustaining the communes was more important than making one big smash."

"It's some kind of desperate measure to fight back?" John suggested.

Bash's expression had darkened. He knew how malicious minds worked better than most did. "Or the monsters are willing to sacrifice their worshippers because they expect to get something even better than a bunch of tiny communes in the end." He looked to me. "What could they do with a big surge of extra energy?"

"I don't know." I curled my fingers into my palms. "When I was in that last city in their realm, where their power was the strongest, I was able to talk to my sister. She wasn't fully present there—even less than we were. They've got her in this world somewhere, but she was able to reach out. She said something about them making her into a 'bridge' for their power, connecting her to the stone… They've had to rely on their cult to give them access to our world so far. Maybe with a big enough push, they could create a permanent passage between their realm and ours."

"That… doesn't sound like a happy development," John said, his jaw tightening.

"No. I'm not sure what the consequences could be, but it might mean they could act on all people, whether we let them in or not, much more freely." The horror of the possibility crawled over me as I said the words. A world where the shrouded folk roamed at will among human beings, preying on them whenever they wanted, drinking in our sunlight… I had to restrain a shudder.

"We need to round up all the cultists we can find as quickly as possible, then," Sherlock said, pushing himself off his stool as if he could stride off to do that personally right now. "If the creatures don't have representatives to act on their behalf before they've opened such a passage, they won't have the chance."

My pulse stuttered, thinking back over everything I'd seen in the shrouded realm. "The city stones gave them energy in their own realm. Those are probably the key. And the most powerful one was in Istanbul. Does Garrett have contacts there? What are the most prominent geometric-styled buildings there? Their police force needs to have people monitoring them, *now*."

John pulled out his phone and hesitated. "It's the middle of the night back in London."

"It doesn't matter. Wake him up. The fiends don't care whether we lose sleep over this. If they're starting this new strategy, that's the first place they'll strike, and one effective blow there might be enough that nothing else we do matters." I hopped off my own stool. "The rest of us should get cleaned up and then head out immediately."

Bash touched my arm. "Was your sister able to tell you where she is?"

"Not exactly." Remembering our distant conversation made my heart squeeze. "I'd bet good money that they have her somewhere near Istanbul, though, if they're trying to use her to make their 'bridge.' Especially since that's where she was able to talk to me. It sounds like that's where we'll be needed most as it is. Come on. Every second could make a difference if you don't want to see these monsters ruling over all of us."

I showered as quickly as I could while getting the oily paste off my skin and out of my hair, and then threw on the dress at the top of my suitcase. There wasn't much in the way of packing to do. I'd only brought a carry-on.

When I wheeled it out into the suite's main room, John had gathered the soiled sheets and the leftover supplies into a box. He set it on the counter as I came over.

"Moran and Sherlock went to use the other rooms rather than waiting, so we can get going sooner," he said, swiping a hand over his head that ruffled his blond hair.

He leaned against one of the stools but didn't quite sit, his walking stick still braced against the floor.

"Sherlock wouldn't let you come along to assist?" I asked in a gently teasing tone. I could only imagine how much the former doctor had been fussing over his friend with the new injuries.

Injuries that were my fault.

John managed a wry smile, but his gaze slid away from me. "He's nothing if not stubborn. And independent. There's a reason I'm not only his best friend but essentially his only one."

And Sherlock was by far John's closest friend—more than friend, really—from what I'd observed. My throat closed up. I groped for the right words to convey the regret I felt without straying into disingenuous remorse. At the very least, I owed it to John to be honest with him. He deserved to make his decisions about how far he took this quest alongside me knowing exactly who I was.

"I'm sorry," I said. "It seemed like a necessary evil to make sure I could save my sister. She had to come first— she still has to. But I didn't like doing it. I didn't *enjoy* the thought of him being hurt, or how you'd feel seeing it."

John met my eyes again. He swallowed audibly, but he didn't look half as angry as he had the right to be. "He's already forgiven you. I guess I should take my cues from him. I— It was your sister you told me about, that first night we slept together during the conference, wasn't it? The person you lost who set you on this path?"

I remembered that conversation with a dull ache in my chest. One of the first small truths I'd allowed myself to share with these men while I was still deceiving them in so many ways.

"Yes," I said. "It's all been for her. The fiends stole her

life, one way or another. I hate them in general, but I mostly hate them for that."

"And you blame yourself for not saving her before they took her."

Exactly how much had Bash told John and Sherlock when they'd turned up here? He wasn't wrong, though.

I lowered my gaze, the discomfort of the admission prickling through me. "Of course I do. I was the only protector she had."

John was silent for several seconds. Then he said, slowly and quietly, "I told you a little before about my older brother, how he died. I could see him going off the rails years before the end. I tried to talk to him, to get him to cut back on the drinking, to take opportunities that would help get his life back on track, but he was difficult to be around. I could have pushed harder, been there more. And that was nothing compared to what you and your sister went through. I don't know, if I had a chance to fix things, to bring him back safe after all… I might go to some pretty horrible lengths to accomplish that."

I had to smile at him, even if the gesture felt bittersweet. "I don't think you'd do anything all that horrible. There's a goodness in you that just shines through, more than I've ever seen in anyone."

"Maybe it's easier to see that from the outside." He considered me. "You don't think you have all that much goodness in *you*, do you? But I've seen plenty."

That remark made me twice as uncomfortable as his comment about blaming myself. "Not so much recently, though," I suggested as a deflection.

"I don't know. There were a lot worse ways you could have pushed someone down a cliff." His mouth slanted crookedly. "Can I ask that you not try out any other ways in the future?"

I let out a rough laugh. "I think I've proven that I'm incapable of really hurting Sherlock even when I intend to."

"You think that's a weakness," John said. "I'd consider it a strength. You were careful with him because you recognize how important he is."

I didn't have to figure out how to answer that, because Bash hustled into the suite at the same instant.

"I've booked our tickets," he said, holding up his phone. "We'll be in Istanbul by the end of the day."

# CHAPTER TEN

*Bash*

We stayed in the car, air conditioning blasting in defiance of Istanbul's late summer heat, peering up at the skyscraper in the city's business district that we'd gotten the address to. I wanted to think that we were barking up the wrong tree, that Jemma's monsters hadn't changed the rules of the game this much, but just looking at the building, a sense of wrongness shivered through me.

The high-rises around it stood straight and for the most part sharply rectangular, with even rows of windows or panes of glass. This one looked as if Picasso had possessed the architect partway through the designing. Floors jutted out here and there at unpredictable intervals. The windows were a hodgepodge of heights and sizes. Even the frame around the front door slanted at a slight but awkward angle.

"Construction was completed just twenty-two months ago," Sherlock said from where he was sitting next to John at the front of the rental car. I hadn't put up an argument about the former doctor taking the wheel after we'd left him behind to go after Jemma into the shrouded realm—it'd seemed only fair. "Most of the funding came from a few individuals associated with the corporation we traced those transfers of Tillhouse's to."

"Tillhouse is locked up now, isn't he?" Jemma said beside me as she contemplated the building.

John nodded. "He couldn't talk his way out of the spectacle we made at the Scotland commune. He's been taken into custody pending trial."

"I doubt he has anything to do with this situation as it currently is," Sherlock put in. "Those transfers would only make up a small amount of the cost of construction, and he passed them on more than five years ago. He may not even have known what the money was going to."

Really, we should be glad for that money, since the transactions had popped up during Garrett's digging—with the help of one of Sherlock's computer expert associates—once we'd focused our attention on Istanbul. Jemma was frowning, though.

"All kinds of people put money into that corporation," she said. "At least some of the others were probably like Tillhouse, under the shrouded folk's sway somehow. They've been extending their influence all over."

I nodded to the building. "Do you think they have a commune set up in there?"

"From the data we've been able to gather so far, the first several floors are legitimate businesses, though of course they're unknowingly funding the owners' plans with their rent," Sherlock said. "The higher floors are all apartments."

"They could have worshippers staying in those apartments, or they could even have changed the layout from the blueprints they submitted to the administrative office and opened those upper floors up more to mimic their usual settlements." Jemma sucked her lower lip under her teeth. "It's definitely going to be a lot harder to storm a secure business establishment than one of those little villages."

"The income they've been able to accumulate means we can't point to any of the usual patterns," John said. "There've been no regular thefts of supplies within the city, for example. I'm not sure we could get a warrant."

Sherlock shifted in his seat. "There are other means of detecting illegal activity. It just may take some time to dig far enough. I have people on it."

"The fiends are already escalating their attacks," Jemma said. She turned away from the window, her face even paler than usual in the bright sunlight that fell across it. "Buildings bombed in Nairobi, Paris, Houston, Delhi, and Moscow in just the last day. Some of those besides Nairobi might be part of their 'wheel' of power. I don't know how much time we have before they do something catastrophic." Her gaze lifted again. "And my sister could very well be up in that tower."

John glanced back at her. "Do you think the shrouded folk will realize we're here? They tracked us pretty well back in London."

"I wouldn't think so, not unless one of them crosses paths with one of us here and is able to recognize us. The mark that one put on Sherlock weeks ago will have faded by now. And even if they have the means to try to trace our movements, we took that last flight under false names." She paused. "On the other hand, the fiends that came after me in their realm may have put the pieces together. They won't know how much I figured out, and they were already worried about how I was interfering with their plans. Whether they know we're in Istanbul or not, they'll be ramping up whatever scheme they have underway even faster."

She motioned to Sherlock. "Make sure your people are checking for the usual signs in the more isolated areas outside the city. It's possible this building serves some other purpose or is some kind of decoy, and the cult's main activities are nearby but on more usual terrain for them."

"I already have that covered," the detective said. "I expect we'll have more answers shortly."

Jemma's expression stayed tensed. "Shortly" wasn't good enough for her in her current state.

"Why don't we scope out the place up close?" I suggested to her. I was eager to take some kind of action too, and having something concrete to do would at least break her out of her fretting. "Just the two of us, so we don't draw too much attention. We can take a look at the businesses and evaluate the building's security at the same time... and I happened to notice there's a pastry café at the back of the first floor."

Jemma shot me a thin flash of a smile. "You know the quickest way to my heart. There's definitely no point in making any plans of our own until we have a clearer sense of our options." She tipped her head to the Londoners. "We'll meet up with you and share observations back at the hotel?"

"Ring us as soon as you're back," John said with a nod.

Jemma had picked up a plain tan headscarf from a shop near the airport after we'd arrived. She pulled it from her shoulders to cover her stark red hair, hiding all but the fringe of it along her forehead. Tucking the ends around her neck, she gestured for me to follow her out of the car.

We ambled over to the skyrise as if we were heading to do our business in no particular rush. Jemma's gaze flicked intently over the front doors and around the entrance as we came in. My military instincts picked up hints in the postures of a few men in suits who lingered near the doorway. They were definitely combat trained, most likely armed.

The elevator only allowed access to the first ten floors with their offices unless you had a keycard for the higher apartments. We'd need to find someone to steal a card from or hack into the control panel. Jemma took us straight up to the tenth floor, I assumed to get a look at security just below the residences.

The tenth floor had a bright modern hall that wouldn't have held any traces of monstrous presence if it wasn't for the faint but chaotic dappling of pastel colors on the wallpaper. Jemma traced her fingers across it as if attempting to connect the dots into some kind of pattern. The monsters would love that.

We strolled along the hall and around the bend, making a show of checking the names on the plaques beside each door as if we had a specific destination in mind. When we turned another corner, the hall stretched on with only blank walls for about thirty feet after the first couple of doors, ending with an exit with a glowing sign —a stairwell for emergencies, I had to guess. Two suits were standing there. As one of them shifted his position to eye us, I caught the shape of a semi-automatic rifle dangling from the hand out of view.

Jemma glanced at both of the offices and shook her head with a rueful laugh. "We must have come the wrong way around," she said in a voice that showed no hint of tension. As we retraced our steps to the elevator, she shot me a pointed look. She hadn't missed the heavy weaponry.

"I think I might have gotten mixed up," she said for the benefit of anyone who'd been marking our travels. "Maybe it was the sixth floor."

We took a similar route around that floor, heading a little more purposefully this time toward the stairwell. Only one guard was staked out at this level, but the bulge of a holster showed at his hip. Whoever had set up this place, they weren't afraid to use some ammunition.

Jemma must have decided we'd be pushing our luck if we meandered around any of the other office floors, so she punched the button for the ground level when we got back on the elevator. "You know," she said, "I'm not sure I'm in the mood for pastries after all. I'm sure we can find something else to hit the spot if we wander a bit."

She was concerned about surveillance in any of the businesses in the building, either manmade or from the shrouded folk. I nodded. "I'm pretty sure I saw a bakery on the way over."

"That should do the trick."

She kept up that mildly upbeat demeanor as we ventured out onto the bustling downtown street. Istanbul's locals were a mix of modern and traditional, much like what I'd seen of the city's structures. Plenty of the people we passed wore clothes that would have fit in just fine on the streets of Manhattan, but here and there women had headscarves like Jemma's wrapped over their hair, and a few wore full loose robes that covered every inch of skin below their chins.

A few blocks along, Jemma glanced through a shop window and grabbed my arm. "It's been too long since I had künefe," she said, her eyes gleaming, and hustled me into the little restaurant.

Within a matter of minutes, we were sitting kitty-corner to each other at a tiny glass table eating a sort of syrupy, crunchy cake, dripping with melted cheese and topped with crumbs of pistachio. I had to admit the combination was mouthwatering, even if desserts weren't my usual food of choice.

Jemma plowed through half of her generous slice with a pleased groan before she said anything about the building we'd investigated.

"They're definitely hiding something up there," she said. "Something they *really* don't want anyone stumbling on. You don't defend stairwells with military grade weapons just for kicks."

"I thought the same thing." I sighed, my enjoyment of the snack fading. "If they were just using the building for income, they wouldn't have brought in that kind of security. It's not going to be fun getting past them. We can't get the jump on them anywhere near as easily as we could with the other communes."

"We *have* to get up there and put an end to whatever they're doing as soon as we can manage it." Jemma jabbed her fork into the cake. "They could be building this 'bridge' to their realm right now—and killing my sister to do it."

"We'll do whatever it takes," I said firmly. Thinking back to what we'd seen of the building... this might be the point where "whatever it takes" included my life. I'd sooner die than let one of those goons shoot down Jemma.

I'd risked my life for her before. I'd gone into more situations than I could count, both while in her employ and before, knowing I might not make it out. For some reason, the thought gave me a twinge of discomfort this time.

No, not just *for some reason*. Because of the other people I'd have been willing to die for, the siblings I'd been having trouble getting out of my mind since Jemma had mentioned them a few days ago.

I should have known Jemma would notice my shift in mood, no matter how slight. She cocked her head at me, pausing after she'd swallowed a bite. "What's the matter, Bash?"

"It's nothing," I said, waving off the question.

She raised her eyebrows at me. "Do you really think I'm going to accept that as an answer? Spit it out. If something's bothering you, it concerns me too."

She said that so easily, taking it for granted that my problems were hers to tackle just as much as hers were mine. God, did I love this woman. I might as well tell her, even though it was such a tiny thing it seemed absurd.

"I was just thinking about my brother and sister," I said. "With everything going on with *your* sister, it's hard not to reflect. Every now and then I wish I'd had a chance to talk to them now that they're grown up. But it's better they don't have to see what I am now, so really, it's a moot point."

Jemma's mouth bent at a pained angle. "Don't be ridiculous. Of course you should talk to them again if you have the chance. They're not going to put you through an interrogation about all your activities in the last however many years first. If it wasn't for you, they might not even be around—I'm sure they remember that. They probably wonder about you all the time."

"I don't know," I said, thinking about the busy lives

they appeared to have when I looked them up, but Jemma made a decisive sound.

"The next time you're back in the States, you'll stop by to at least say hello," she said. "Promise me that."

"Is that an order?"

"It is. You haven't let me down so far—don't start now."

Her tone was lightly teasing, but her gaze was serious. It occurred to me that she'd specifically said when *I* was back in the US, as if there was much chance I'd be going there on my own instead of it being a matter of "we."

Maybe she didn't think we *would* be going back together. The same instincts that had helped me identify the building's guards prickled up my back as I studied her.

She'd seen the same set-up I had. She was talking about bursting in there and taking down the cult immediately. I'd heard how she'd talked about her sister— I could see the signs of tension in her now, running through her shoulders and the flex of her jaw.

She was bracing herself, preparing herself. To go charging in there and screw herself over to save her sister? She'd probably see that as a fair trade after all the years her sister had been held.

It didn't sound like a fair trade to me. My own shoulders stiffened at the thought.

"You should have the chance to do a lot of things after this too," I said in a low voice. "To see your sister recover, to get to know her all over again, to introduce her to the real world. To enjoy this world without the shrouded folk always in the background."

She smiled, but it still looked pained. "We'll see. First things first."

I knew better than to push the issue, but I couldn't

shake the feeling that I had to do something to make sure she knew how many options *she* had.

It might be more than I could manage on my own. I knew her and I loved her, but Jemma was far from simple. It wasn't any surprise she might need more than one man to fulfill all her needs, was it? Between me and each member of the trio, we all offered something different—and she deserved to have all of that. We just had to make sure she saw it that way.

For the first time, picturing her with the other guys didn't make my chest clench up even slightly. I wanted her to have everything she needed, and the part I offered mattered just as much as anyone else's.

I just wasn't sure if she realized that what she offered us was something pretty spectacular too. That the life she had, no matter who she'd had to leave behind or what she'd been through, was damn well worth holding on to if she possibly could.

# CHAPTER ELEVEN

*Jemma*

I sat tensed in the hotel chair for a minute or so before I initiated the video chat to Garrett's number in London. Traffic rumbled by on the road a few floors below, and a warm breeze carried through the open window, where a roaming cat had come to sprawl on the wide ledge in the last of the afternoon sun.

There shouldn't have been anything stressful about the situation. I'd talked to the detective inspector hundreds of times, many of which while he'd been incredibly suspicious of me. His opinion of me shouldn't have mattered all that much anyway.

But on some level it did. I'd let John and Sherlock handle the communications with him before now. Part of me hadn't wanted to face how he'd react the first time we spoke after my horrible ruse on the mountain. I might have kept up that policy if it hadn't started to feel embarrassingly cowardly.

And if I hadn't become increasingly sure that this

conversation might not be just the first since that incident, but also my last chance to talk to him at all.

I'd texted him ahead of time to ask if he was up for the video call, so Garrett was expecting me. The app connected within a few seconds. The video link kicked in to reveal his boyishly handsome face, his dark brown eyes as intense as ever and what I could see of his wiry form as tense as I felt.

"Jemma," he said in an unreadable voice. He wasn't so much emotionless as showing so many hints of conflicting emotions that I couldn't tell which was winning out. I supposed that was to be expected from a man trying to come to grips with the fact that the woman he'd believed he loved had been willing to nearly murder a long-time friend in front of him.

"Garrett," I replied in acknowledgment. "I thought I'd do the check-in this time, find out any news you have from your channels about the cult's activities."

He turned his head as if to look at something else on his desk. "Right. We've had several more reports come in today of property damage attempted or accomplished. The local police did manage to apprehend a few of the groups before they could go through with their plans. Sherlock mentioned Tehran—that was one of the spots— as well as Vancouver, Atlanta, Madrid, Algiers, and Singapore. Nothing in Istanbul yet. No changes to the MO we've seen so far."

"No bystanders have been hurt?"

"There've been some cuts, burns, and bruises, but nothing critical, thankfully." His gaze came back to me. Even through the computer speakers, I could hear his voice flatten slightly. "I guess there's been a lot of luck going around in general in that respect."

The subtle reference to Sherlock's fall made my throat tighten. I did my best to keep my own tone casual. "You're angry with me. That's reasonable."

He sighed. "I don't know what I am. I can't say it never occurred to me that you were capable of something like that. I'd imagine you've done worse to other people in the past."

He'd seen the results of my efforts in the communes, the guards I'd dispatched. There were plenty of people I *had* killed, without any remorse. But… "You never had to see it. It was never anyone like you."

"Sherlock seems to think the way you handled it makes everything okay. I've never been able to completely wrap my head around how that mind of his works." Garrett shook his head with a small, slanted smile.

"Sherlock is certainly a unique individual." I drew in a breath and said what I really needed to say while I had the chance to say it. "If what happened changes the way you see me, I understand that. It's all right if you can't forgive me. I knew I was taking that chance."

Garrett blinked, clearly started. "Jemma—"

"You didn't make any promises," I barreled on, "and even if you had, I wouldn't hold you to them after something like that. You don't owe me anything. It really is all right. I am what I am, and I never went out of my way to drive home exactly what that means, so of course you couldn't have known everything I was capable of."

Garrett still looked puzzled. "Why are you saying all this?"

I groped for the best explanation, not even sure I could fully explain it to myself. *Because I needed to. Because I don't want to leave any more carnage in my wake than I have to. Because I may not be a "good" person, but I won't be a monster either.*

"Because I know what you're like. You're already carrying around enough guilt over ways you feel you've failed people. I'd rather not add to the pile."

He paused. His next words came out slow and careful, his gaze studying me through the screen. "And what makes you so sure I'm going to see my association with you as a failure?"

"I don't take you for the kind of person who'd tell me what you did lightly," I said. "You meant it for the woman you'd seen, but you hadn't seen everything. So... so it's all right."

Bash would still love me, because he'd known what I was all along. Sherlock and John had never expressed that deep a sentiment—Sherlock had once referred to his feelings for me as more along the lines of fascination, and I'd imagine that still applied. Garrett had put his heart on the line in a way I'd never expected and yet couldn't help feeling partly responsible for.

Garrett's expression had turned both shrewd and sad in a way I wasn't entirely sure I liked. "It would be easier for you too if I was just angry about it, if I didn't want anything else to do with you, wouldn't it?"

I opened my mouth and closed it again before I could form a suitable response. "I'm not sure what you mean. I simply wanted you to know—"

His smile came back, rueful this time... and maybe even a little fond. "You're forgetting that I do actually know you pretty well at this point, Jemma. The incident in Scotland showed a lot of things, one of which was how much in the habit you are of pushing people away— sometimes literally—when you're about to run into some horrifying situation. What are you trying to keep me out of?"

That wasn't at all the idea I'd wanted him to come away with. I summoned the haughtiest tone I had in me. "You're already apprised of as much of the situation here as we know about it. And I'd hardly need to push you away when you're already on the other side of the continent, would I?"

He didn't rise to the bait. "I think it'd be better if we waited to finish this conversation in person. I assume from what you just said that there's nothing else I should know about things in Istanbul?"

Not that I wanted him to know. I was supposed to convene with Bash, Sherlock, and John over dinner to discuss any new developments, but one of them could fill the detective inspector in as they saw fit. "You assume correctly. Garrett, there's really—"

He held up his hand with a calm firmness I hadn't often seen in him before. His experiences over the last few months had obviously changed him, perhaps in more ways than I'd realized. "When we can talk in person. It was good to hear from you, Jemma."

He ended the call without giving me the chance to respond. That showed some nerve right there. I glared at the computer screen for a few seconds before snapping the laptop shut. Something about his words and the way he'd said them left me with an uneasy impression, but I couldn't put my finger on exactly what I was worried about.

By the end of tomorrow, it wasn't likely to matter anyway.

When I slipped into Sherlock and John's shared suite a short time later, Bash had already arrived with the food:

lamb dumplings slathered in yogurt sauce that set my mouth watering with one whiff of their garlicky smell. As much as I loved my sweets, I could appreciate a damn good main course.

As we ate, we also talked business, of course.

"The security personnel you saw in the tower appear to be either individual hires or supplied from within the cult," Sherlock said, checking over the notes on his phone in between dumplings. "There's no record of any security company being contracted to work there. Most likely cult members, I would suspect."

"So would I." That would fit with the way they'd protected their other communes—keeping it in the "family," so to speak.

"That means it won't be easy to displace them the way we did with the gallery heist in London," John remarked with a frown.

"We couldn't really expect it to be all that easy," I pointed out.

"What about the architecture of the building itself?" Bash asked. "Any points of access we missed there?"

Sherlock shook his head. "There is the elevator shaft, of course, with the natural dangers that comes with—and the possibility of being caught accessing it."

"We don't know which of all those upper floors we'd need to get to anyway," John said. "And they're bound to have even tighter security there, aren't they?"

I glanced at Bash. "Where you able to get in touch with that contact you thought might be able to help us with that?"

"I'm meeting with him after dinner and we'll see what we can make out first thing in the morning." He turned to the other men. "We're going to attempt to get a better sense of the higher floors using a drone with a camera to peer through the windows. Not the most elegant solution ever…"

"But we'll take what we can get." John brightened. "That's some progress, anyway. The local police appear willing to lend a hand if we can frame the situation properly. They've been keeping a close watch on the buildings that seemed the most likely targets—if the cult was planning a move here, I'd imagine the police presence has dissuaded them."

For now. I chewed my last dumpling, lingering in the rich savory flavors for as long as I could extend the sensation before I had to swallow. "Tomorrow, as soon as you have the footage, I want to look it over," I said to Bash. Whatever glimpses he and his contact managed to obtain might be all the additional guidance I needed. I'd already made a morning appointment of my own to pick up some firepower.

He bowed his head with a playful flourish. "I both hear and grant you your requests." He checked at the time and got to his feet. "I'd better not make him wait. He seemed a little nervous about the whole thing."

As he let himself out, Sherlock rose and made an attempt at clearing the takeout garbage from the table, rather awkwardly with his one arm in its cast. John swept in before he'd gathered more than a few pieces.

"You never know when to give yourself a rest, do you?" he said, chidingly but with unmistakable affection.

Sherlock grimaced at his friend as the other man took over, but he rested a hand on John's shoulder in what could only be called a caress before he stepped back. John shot him a smile filled with warmth and a spark of desire.

Watching them and the small but certain intimacies

they'd become comfortable with melted most of the uneasiness I'd been left with after the call with Garrett. If John was right about the "goodness" in me, then the best thing I'd probably done outside of however much progress I'd made toward ridding the world of the shrouded folk was in evidence right in front of me. The two men hadn't even admitted their mutual attraction to themselves when I'd first met them, and now they were all but flirting right in front of me.

They would be fine without me—at least, I thought so. It couldn't hurt anything to solidify that bond even further while I was still here, could it? One final night with these two men I'd become rather fond of myself... A last hurrah would make tomorrow's plans that much easier.

When John returned to the table, I folded my arms over my chest. "I don't seem to see anything like dessert around here."

Sherlock chuckled. "A horrendous oversight. Blame your man. He brought the food."

"He's not here anymore, though. But I think there might be other ways that hunger could be satisfied."

John's gaze turned heated at the suggestive lilt to my voice, but he didn't step any closer, just gave his walking stick a sly swivel. "And what would those be?"

He was still a little more hesitant with me than he might have been before Sherlock's fall at my hands. I eased up to him and lay those hands on his chest—carefully, so that he could easily pull away if this wasn't what he wanted at all. "I think you could make a reasonable guess."

He raised his arm and traced his fingers over my hair as if refamiliarizing himself with the feel of me. Making sure I was the woman he thought he saw. My pulse stuttered as I waited, but whatever he was thinking, whatever he was remembering, a moment later he lowered his head to bring his lips to mine.

He kissed me the way only John Watson could, gently but intently, taking and offering of himself in equal portions. It'd been over a week since I'd last gotten to experience the sensation, and I hadn't realized how much I'd missed it. I kissed him back with plenty of enthusiasm but not too forcefully, still careful of scaring him off.

A hand, a little stiff from the plaster casing that crossed the palm, settled on my waist from behind. Sherlock brushed my hair to the side and ran his finger over one of the sensitive spots he'd previously discovered on my neck. I swayed against him encouragingly, and he pressed his mouth to the same spot, no doubt marking the hitch of my breath with analytical precision. The fact that he'd moved to join us at all without a conversation to justify this indulgence was a big step all on its own.

I gripped John's shirt and reached back to stroke my hand down Sherlock's side at the same time. As John kissed me more deeply, he brushed his fingers over my hair again and then teased them over Sherlock's messy curls as well. Sherlock raised his head with a ripple of hot breath over my skin. John shifted from me to his friend in one smooth movement, planting a kiss on Sherlock over my shoulder.

I couldn't say which turned me on more: having both of these men's attentions focused on me or watching them attend to each other. Especially when I got to stay part of the action. John's hand trailed down over my blouse to fondle my breast, and Sherlock pressed himself against my ass with a firm grasp on my hip, and it felt as if all three of us might melt together into a mass of bliss.

For a few minutes, I was content to simply stoke those flames. The men alternated between branding my lips and neck with their mouths and claiming each other. I lost track of whose hand was sparking pleasure where. But at the shift of John's weight on his feet, my concern for his injured leg leapt into sharper awareness.

I kissed him once more, hard now that I was surer of him, and drew back an inch. "Let's take this to my room. I have the… necessary supplies there."

The flush of John's cheeks and the squeeze of Sherlock's fingers on my thigh was agreement enough. We managed to disentangle ourselves from each other long enough to make the short trip across the hall. I grabbed a couple of condoms out of my suitcase, paused, and tossed a small bottle of lube onto the bedside table too. It might come in handy. An idea was starting to unfurl through my mind that I thought we'd all enjoy very much.

I raised my arms, and John took the cue to pull off my blouse. Sherlock unhooked my bra a second later. As John lowered his head to chart a path across my breasts, I fumbled with the buttons on the other man's shirt. A gasp slipped from my lips as John scraped his teeth across one of my nipples with a jolt of pleasure.

"Naughty," I said, not at all a complaint, and he chuckled.

Sherlock tossed his shirt aside and captured my mouth with a demanding kiss, and John sank lower, onto his knees. He might not be able to handle an operating table, but his fingers were still nimble enough to make short work of my slacks and panties. When he brought his hot mouth to my sex, fire flooded me up to the top of my head and down to my toes.

I moaned against Sherlock's lips, and he took the opportunity to test my tongue with his. As ours dueled above, John slicked his tongue over my clit and lower. A fresh wave of bliss shivered through me with an instinctive rock of my hips.

John added a finger, sliding it along my slit and then in with a pleased hum at the feel of my arousal. Sherlock cupped my breast, tweaking the nipple, and John suckled me harder. Faster than I'd expected, ecstasy rolled over me.

As the aftershock rippled through me, John looked up with a beaming smile. So goddamned adorable. I wanted him gasping with pleasure too—both of them, so satisfied they never forgot this night, never looked back on it with anything but happiness.

"Get up here," I growled, tugging him to his feet, and undid his fly before he'd even finished straightening up. I drew him onto the bed with me, Sherlock following beside us. He ran his hand down John's thighs as he helped me remove the other man's slacks, and a different sort of bliss came over John's face.

Oh, yes, I had to see that these two completely fulfilled their potential.

John grabbed one of the condoms and slicked it on at light speed. I raised my hips, and that was all the encouragement he needed to plunge into me. He kissed me, then Sherlock, and then Sherlock kissed me. The doctor moved with leisurely thrusts, patiently building to our joint release.

Which I intended to be a release for all of us… of all sorts of passions. I traced my hand down John's back and pushed myself up with my other arm so I could grip his ass. The sharper angle let his cock hit an even more perfect spot inside me. My breath broke, and it took me a second to remember my aim.

I eased my fingers to the crease of his ass. "It feels fucking amazing having someone inside you," I said by his ear. "Imagine if you could experience that too."

A quiver ran through John's body when I teased my fingertips into that crease and around the sensitive ring there. Next to us, Sherlock had gone abruptly still, his hand lingering on my breast, his gaze following the movement of my hand. He was sharp enough to know where I was going with this from just that comment.

Apparently John was too. His eyes widened slightly and then closed with a groan as I dipped a finger right inside him much as he'd done to me earlier. His gaze slid to Sherlock as he answered me. "I might have thought about that before."

"Mmm. Somehow I suspect you're not the only one." I kissed John and then gave Sherlock an amused smile. "Am I right in assuming you've done your research?"

A hint of pink colored the detective's cheeks, but he owned up to it. "Considering how things had been developing, it seemed reasonable to investigate all the possibilities."

I had to laugh. "You still need to work on your dirty talk. Give me a hand, then. And the lube."

He opened the bottle and smeared some of the stuff on his own fingers before passing it to me. Carefully, he brought his hand to the same spot I'd marked, watching John's expression carefully the whole time. The doctor let out a shaky breath. His thrusts had turned shallow, but I wasn't worried about my own satisfaction right now.

I drew my hand back, sinking down on the bed again

now that Sherlock had gotten a start. John kissed me a little wildly. "Sherlock," he said in a strained voice.

The other man wet his lips, looking thrilled and hesitant at the same time. "Are you sure this is what you want?" he said in the gentlest voice I'd ever heard him use.

"God, yes." John paused, glancing back at him. "Do you?"

The color in Sherlock's face deepened. "I have been curious how the sensation would compare."

"Oh my God," I muttered in mock-frustration, suppressing another laugh. Better that I didn't push them toward the act any more than I already had. If they were going to keep on their journey together without me, they needed to be sure they'd gotten onto the path of their own accord.

Thankfully, Sherlock didn't need more confirmation. He slicked more of the gel over his cock and bowed over John as he eased inside with the utmost care. John's limbs trembled against mine, but I could tell from the catch in his throat that his reaction was all pleasure. He groaned again as Sherlock grasped his thigh, getting settled into his position. Then John picked up his pace inside me.

His body continued to shake with what must have been a symphony of sensations, bucking forward into me and back to take in Sherlock. With the first few strokes, Sherlock groaned as well. The detective's hand dropped from John's thigh to caress mine before resuming its braced position. The rhythm of their rising panting only stoked my own arousal.

I arched into John's thrusts, joining that rhythm. Becoming part of that mass of bliss all over again. John made a strangled sound, his mouth mashing against mine, and if he'd come before I hit my peak, I wouldn't even have minded. But as his hips jerked toward me with fraying control, I found myself cast across the last short distance to the edge. His cock filled me once more, and I was soaring, gasping, holding onto him as he spilled himself in me.

Sherlock let out a ragged curse, and I knew he'd followed with us. He hugged John even more tightly to him for a few moments. Then they sagged down on either side of me, their arms looping over my torso to embrace each other as well as me.

In that combined embrace, a tight, unfamiliar ache formed behind my breastbone. I nuzzled John's face and tipped my head toward Sherlock for one last kiss.

I'd started this for their benefit at least as much as mine, but it suddenly felt vital that I say something more than I had before.

"I'm glad I barged into your lives, you know," I said quietly. "I'm glad you both tracked me down after I took off on you—and Garrett too. I didn't think I needed more than I had, but you opened up so many possibilities… So many things I didn't know I could have."

John pulled himself a little closer to me and kissed my bare shoulder. "You know we could say the exact same thing to you, don't you?"

"I'll admit I find it difficult now to imagine a life that didn't include Jemma Moriarty," Sherlock said with a wry smile.

The ache turned into a pang, but I ignored that. I'd swept into their lives, and perhaps I'd changed them, but those changes were in place now. They could move on without me when they had to. And I was lucky to have gotten to experience this for as long as I had.

# CHAPTER TWELVE

*Jemma*

I thought I'd have that last day to enjoy all there was to take pleasure in within the world. Pick up my munitions, meet with Bash to see the drone photos he'd gotten, solidify my strategy, and then think about anything but the task ahead for the hours remaining until the sun set.

Unfortunately, the cult of the shrouded folk decided not to cooperate with that plan.

I'd just picked up the weapons order I'd made. I was walking along the warm, arid street amid Istanbul's morning pedestrians, the thick canvas bag slung over my shoulder with a few knobby protrusions poking into my back, when an immense cracking sound split the air from somewhere in the distance. I spun around in time to see a plume of smoke streaking up over the business quarter.

My back stiffened. Despite all our precautions here and the cops' willingness to help, the cult must have managed to strike. If they were willing to sacrifice some of their local people for the effort today… did that mean they were close to their goal?

As I hurried back to the modest hotel, my heart thumped faster. There'd be fewer people in the urban commune right now. They'd be distracted as they tracked the results of their efforts. Going now might give me more of an advantage than going at night. It wasn't even that sunny out anyway, the sky hazed with a thin layer of pale cloud.

I'd been given a chance. I had to take it.

I ducked into my hotel room and stashed the bag of weapons on the shelf in the closet. Bash had better be back with those photographs. I'd get him to hand them over and study them while I dressed and armed myself for the mission.

Before I could leave, I'd need to find some quest to send the guys on so they wouldn't be around to see me heading off. That shouldn't be too hard. I could figure that out while I was studying the photographs too.

I threw open the door to hustle to Bash's room and froze at the sight of the man just outside.

Well, actually there were four men in the hall, but it was only the one right in front of me that made my pulse stutter. Garrett's hand had been raised to knock, his jaw set at a familiar determined angle. He startled briefly at the swing of the door. I stared at him, momentarily lost for words, only vaguely registering the rest of the London trio and my right-hand man in their semi-circle behind him.

"What are *you* doing here?" I finally managed.

The detective inspector gave me a grim but not unfriendly smile. "Hello to you too, Jemma."

"Fine. Hello, greetings, good day, isn't the weather lovely, I hope the family's well, etc." I waved my hand in the air. "Now answer the question—what the hell are you doing here? Aren't you supposed to be coordinating a global cult takedown from Scotland Yard?" It was easier to focus on that than to wonder how this fit in with our fraught conversation last night. I'd considered this loose end tied up, but here he was in the flesh, impossible to ignore.

"I'd been wanting to join the efforts here since I first heard what you all were up to," Garrett said. "After our chat yesterday, I decided it was time to get on with that. There was a seat available on an overnight flight direct."

"Wonderful. And now you're here. You're all here." I lifted my gaze to really take in the rest of the guys. Apprehension trickled through me. "Why did you all come over to my room? Is there a problem? I saw some kind of attack happened downtown—it looked about the same as the others, but if it was more serious—"

"We're not here about the bombing downtown," Sherlock said evenly. "Although that is a concern. We're here because it only took a short discussion for us to determine that we've all seen reason for concern in *your* behavior."

"My— What is this? Some kind of intervention?" I narrowed my eyes at the bunch of them, but even Bash held firm. "I don't need one."

"We'd just like to talk," John said softly. "Would you come over to our suite, just for a little while?"

"We can look over the footage the drone was able to capture too," Bash said. "It's probably best if everyone sees that."

I didn't think so. I didn't want any of these four

setting one foot in that building again. But obviously I wasn't getting much say in the matter.

I let out my breath in a huff and stepped out of my room. "All right. Talk away." I didn't have to tell them anything I didn't want to. It wasn't as if I had a shortage of practice dodging private topics.

The table in John and Sherlock's suite wasn't really big enough to comfortably seat five, so we ended up in the sitting area with its long narrow sofa and two arch-backed armchairs. I dropped down at the end of the sofa where it wouldn't feel as much as if I was in the hot seat. Bash sat beside me, studying my face.

He knew me better than any of them. Of course, I'd also expected that he knew better than to share any more sensitive observations he made with the rest of them. They were forming a regular conspiracy, apparently.

Garrett sat in the armchair closest to me, and John and Sherlock took the spots at the other end of the living room. For a few seconds, none of them seemed to know how to start. Then Bash said, in his low smooth voice, "Where did you go this morning, Mori?"

If he'd noticed I'd left, he might have noticed my cargo coming back, so I couldn't offer too obvious a lie. "I was just picking up some supplies that might help us take on the cult. I'm not going to sit around twiddling my thumbs while the rest of you do all the work."

"What kind of supplies?" Sherlock asked.

I gave a casual shrug. "Pieces that'll mess with the shrouded folk's energy. Equipment for climbing the elevator shaft. That sort of thing. Why was an interrogation about that necessary?"

I intended to glance around at them with an air of confusion, but when my eyes caught on Garrett's, I found it hard to look away. He was watching me with that almost sad air I'd sensed from him briefly through the computer screen yesterday.

"And what's your plan, Jemma?" he said. "What part do we play in it?"

"I assumed we'd figure that out once we had a look at Bash's pictures." Impatience wriggled through me. If I was going to take advantage of the cult's distraction, I needed to get out there soon.

"The thing is," John said, leaning forward on the sofa so he could see me better, "we've *all* gotten the impression in the last couple days that you're preparing for something you're not including any of us in. That you've been saying good-bye in your own way. And I don't think I'm convinced yet that we were wrong."

My instincts screamed for me to get out of this conversation immediately, but I couldn't do much of anything without Bash's data. I kept my expression placid. "I'm sorry if I came across that way."

Sherlock let out a sound like a restrained snort. "I'd imagine you are sorry you *came across* that way, since you'd obviously rather we hadn't caught on. Haven't you dashed off on your own enough times, Jemma? We've accomplished the most when we've pooled our resources and talents, not when you've gone rogue."

A wave of exhaustion washed over me. What was the point of continuing to dissemble when even Sherlock was sure of my intentions—and right? If I'd revealed too many of my cards, he wasn't going to let this go. And I wasn't going to get to my goal by pushing him or anyone else in the room to their theoretical deaths this time.

"This is different," I said. "This is the fiends' ultimate plan. This is the center of their influence in our world.

This is my *sister*. If it's just me, I know I can get in, I can pretend to negotiate with them—I can save her and destroy everything else they're working toward. That's all that matters."

Bash's mouth twisted, but he didn't look surprised. "You're not counting on getting back out."

"That's where there's the most chance for failure. If I just go and get it done, then that's… that's enough. The rest doesn't matter. If I start pulling my punches because I'm worried about coming out alive, then I'm screwed." I gave each of the men around me a sharp look. "But that's *my* sacrifice to make. In a way, it's the sacrifice I was supposed to make ten years ago, only it's on my terms this time, and I get to make them pay. That's the most I could ask for. It's *more* than I expected to get to ask for." I'd never thought I'd rescue my sister along with avenging her.

"But what if you could have even more than that?" John said. "You haven't given us a chance to strategize. We could save her and destroy them, and you'd still get the rest of your life."

"Or you might all end up dead instead of it only being me. We might not pull off anything. The more complicated the plan, the harder it is to pull it off."

"So you're going to push yourself off a cliff this time," Garrett said.

My gaze jerked to him. "That seems a lot more fair, don't you think?"

He looked straight back at me unwaveringly. "Wouldn't you rather have a future—with your sister? With us?"

My chest constricted. "What does that even mean? Whatever we've had, it's all been around this quest to get rid of the shrouded folk. It'd fall apart as soon as that's over anyway."

John raised his eyebrows. "Because you wouldn't want it anymore, or because you assume that we wouldn't?"

"I—" I started, groping through words through the rust of emotion that question provoked, and Bash took my hand in his, twining our fingers together.

"We're not asking you to give up your quest, Mori. None of us would do that. Believe me, I wouldn't be sitting here with this bunch if I didn't know they respected you that much. We just want you to give the future a chance. To give yourself a chance. To give *us* a chance to really be something other than a monster-fighting unit. All we want is the chance to see if there's a feasible way we can take these creatures down that doesn't end with you dying. And if there is… wouldn't you take that route?"

When he put it that plainly, when they all waited for my response the way they were right now with that air of hope, something twisted inside me. To imagine being as satisfied as I'd found myself in the last few months, challenged and invigorated and adored, even after the menace of the shrouded folk was no longer looming over us… That sounded like fucking heaven.

It also sounded so impossible that my heart shuttered at the thought.

I gripped Bash's hand. "I know you'd be here for me no matter what. You always have been. But…" I looked around at the London trio again. "Even if we banish the shrouded folk from this world forever, I'm not going to transform in a shower of pixie dust into some kind of fair maiden. You've seen what I am. I'm still going to be that woman. I'll break the law, I'll twist what you see as morality, I'll be most at home on the side of darkness. It won't be as easy to ignore when we're not up against a threat to all humanity."

Sherlock gave a dry laugh. "Do you think we'd want a fair maiden? The way you are, the way you think—it's brilliant. If I'd dispute some of the details, we could hash that out in good time. I've met plenty of 'fair maidens' in my time, and none of them had the slightest appeal to me."

"Because you're insane," I informed him, thinking back of John's remark in the Tokyo hotel.

The detective's lips curled into a smile I couldn't call anything other than a smirk.

"If he's insane, then we all must be," Garrett said. "I… I can't imagine you being any other way, Jemma. And I can't imagine not being part of whatever dark and brilliant life you'd lead on the other side of this, if you'd still have me."

His voice dipped with the last part, as if he really thought *I* might reject *him* after I'd gone to such lengths last night to give him an out.

"You can say whatever you want about yourself," John added. "But I know what I've seen. And what I've seen in the time I've spent around you is not only brilliance but more generosity than just about anyone I can think of. Like Sherlock said, the details can be worked out later. I want to work them out. We work well together, the five of us. I want to see what we can be when there isn't some urgent threat for us to fight."

The ache that'd come over me lying between him and Sherlock yesterday expanded through my chest.

I believed they meant all this now. I didn't know if I could believe they'd still mean it when they were faced with the reality. But… these were the smartest and most devoted men I'd ever met. If anyone could say what they were saying, it was them.

And hell, I *wanted* to believe them, so fucking badly.

Really talking through a plan, considering all the possibilities, and letting them be a part of it would be more complicated than sneaking into the building alone and blasting the cult and their instruments to smithereens. It would be harder and more painful, with the lives of these four men to worry about in ways I didn't quite worry about my own. But damn it, I wanted that chance.

I didn't let myself think about what I might be owed very often. Didn't I owe it to *them* to give it a try, though, after all the faith they'd just offered me?

I dragged in a ragged breath, and the words spilled out. "All right. Let's see what we can come up with when we put our heads together. But we need to get this plan worked out *fast*."

# CHAPTER THIRTEEN

*Sherlock*

The commander from the local police was one of the more agreeable law enforcement officers I'd spoken to in my time.

"We appreciate you lending your wisdom and experience to this situation, Mr. Holmes and Mr. Lestrade," the portly fellow said as he flipped through the images of the dark-paned office building that had been damaged by more of the cult's homemade bombs. "There've been some political problems in this country over the years, but we haven't seen anything quite like this."

"The perpetrators you brought in—could you confirm them as local citizens?" Garrett asked, leaning forward to study the photographs.

"None of the four of them had any sort of ID, and they've refused to give even their names. We were able to match one of the men to a record using photo recognition, but he hasn't shown any activity under that identity in several years. The others we couldn't find matches for at all."

"From what we understand, it isn't unusual for this cult to keep to themselves and handle even births within their communes without involving any of the standard procedures," I said, but Garrett was frowning.

"Only four?" he said. "Were there others on the scene who managed to escape?"

The commander shook his head. "All the witness accounts mention only the individuals we brought in. They made no attempt to flee. It appeared to my officers that they wanted to extend the amount of time they could be carrying out their strange ritual with the blood and so on for as long as possible."

I glanced at the detective inspector. That detail hadn't stood out to me, but Garrett had been much more heavily involved in tracking the international incidents committed by these people. He might not connect the dots quite so swiftly as I preferred to, but he was still sharp enough that having him here was a benefit.

"Were there more present for the other bombings?" I asked.

Garrett nodded. "Generally eight to ten. Occasionally even more than that. They've never needed that much assistance to carry out the explosive aspect, so I'd assumed they wanted as many people involved in the ritual as possible for maximum effect."

"So it's odd that they'd hold back here. Unless they're saving their manpower for future efforts." Ah, yes, I could see why that possibility would disturb him. It rather disturbed me.

The cultists themselves were difficult to predict given their isolation from regular society. The "gods" they worshipped were inscrutable on an even higher level. With an ordinary criminal, I might have made a reasonably accurate guess as to their next move. In this case, I could think of several equally likely scenarios… and I recognized that the outcome might be none of those.

"Exactly." Garrett motioned to the commander. "How many of your people can you have monitoring activity in the business district and around those other buildings we've pointed out as likely targets? I know it's a lot of territory to cover, but the change in the pattern makes me concerned about what else this group might have up their sleeve."

"We've implemented regular patrols and kept the officers informed of the signs to watch for. After this crime, I can justify bringing in some reinforcements from farther abroad. We've also spoken with the private security present at most of the buildings to help them prepare. Unfortunately in this current case, the perpetrators were able to disguise their intentions until it was too late."

"This particular building didn't have a bag search or similar security protocol," I said to confirm.

"No, it hadn't been necessary."

"That's probably why they picked that one," Garrett said. "Any of the other buildings meeting the usual criteria that don't search visitors should add that to their protocol for the time being if at all possible. If not, I suppose doubling the police and other security presence at those locations would have some benefit."

Exactly what I would have suggested. I gave my colleague an approving smile. "I fully agree with that approach."

"I'll see what I can do," the commander said. "People

often complain about increased monitoring, but when we have an example of what we're trying to guard against, it may be easier to convince them."

"There were no casualties from the bombs, were there?" Garrett checked.

"We had several civilians hospitalized, but none of the injuries have been serious. The perpetrators seemed to be focused on hurting the building more than anyone in it."

"That fits with what we've seen elsewhere, at least. Have you been able to find any further information on the owners or inhabitants of the building we've identified as the likely local cult headquarters?"

"Nothing beyond what we were already able to produce. If we come up with something else, I'll be in touch immediately."

"We appreciate that," I said, standing. The meeting had obviously fulfilled its usefulness. Time to move on. It wasn't likely the police could discover more using their official channels than my internet-savvy connections had been able to procure for us.

"I don't like it," Garrett said as we left the police building. "I guess it's good in the short term that the cult hasn't made a larger effort here, but I don't think we'd want to find out how they plan on escalating the situation."

"Agreed. Well, we're pulling together our own plans as swiftly as we can. They won't be able to anticipate everything *we'll* do."

I paused, an unexpected compulsion coming over me. Perhaps it was simply brought on by our conversation with Jemma earlier this morning—by seeing how thoroughly even her genius mind had been able to convince her that in spite of all available evidence, we wouldn't have any interest in her once this case was over.

To ensure some things were understood, you couldn't rely on actions and observations. The words themselves needed to be said. And Jemma was hardly the only member of our team I valued.

"You've done solid work handling the communes abroad," I said to Garrett. "There's a lot of data to sort through and an abundance of people to keep organized, and you've stepped up admirably while we were occupied with our more specific quest."

I knew at once that putting my respect into words had been worthwhile from the brightening of the other man's expression. Perhaps I'd been rather harder on him than he'd deserved at times in the past. Although if I hadn't been, he might not have been able to step up the way he had now, so no point in dwelling on that.

"High praise from the great Sherlock Holmes," he said in an amused tone, but his smile showed how much he genuinely appreciated it. "Unless that's a hint that I should get back to my post in London?"

"No, not at all. At this point, I think this is the best place you could be. There aren't many people in this world I fully trust, and I'd like to have all of them on hand for what may be the final confrontation with these… monsters."

"You're still not totally comfortable with the idea of them, are you?" Garrett said. "It's not as if we can deny their existence."

"No. I'd just greatly prefer it if they didn't exist at all."

My phone vibrated with a text alert. I stopped on the sidewalk to check it and immediately looked up to search for a cab. "John has some leads on the equipment we might use. He wants to go over it with me. Were you still going to see if you can get anything out of the cultists they have in custody?"

"As much good as it might do us. None of them elsewhere have been much for talking, but I'll see if I can find some leverage to apply. If we could get them to talk, it'd certainly be worth the effort."

"It would." I gave him an awkward clap on the shoulder that I meant as a friendly gesture and waved to the cab I'd spotted. "We can reconvene to discuss our progress at the hotel in a few hours."

John was waiting for me at a table outside a café not far from the hotel. At my first glimpse of him, I allowed myself the momentary indulgence of noticing the gleam of the sunlight in his bright hair, the sparkle in his hazel eyes that looked green when he wore that moss-colored shirt. As ridiculous as it seemed to care about those aspects of him, it also seemed ridiculous that somehow I'd gone years before without noticing them at all.

Or perhaps I had and some part of me had simply refused to acknowledge it.

He'd already procured himself a lemonade with a sprig of mint and a plate of small pastries that gave off a buttery scent as I sat down across from him.

"Picking up Jemma's tastes in cuisine, are you?" I said wryly.

He nudged the plate toward me. "They're really very satisfying. Might as well enjoy the local dishes while we're here."

I bit into one and found it wasn't as sweet as I expected, filled with a fruity tartness and a hint of wine that was quite enjoyable. The rest of that pastry disappeared into my mouth in a flash. It had been rather a long time since breakfast. Mind and body needed their fuel.

"What did you come up with?" I asked my friend.

He had a journal on the table beside him. As I ate another pastry, he flipped it open. "I focused mostly on what you said about your experiences in the shrouded realm and how elements of the environment affected you. If we're going to create the opposite effect so the shrouded folk who might be hanging around the tower can't interfere, we'll want to focus on opposite sorts of stimuli, right? Patterns and orderly sensations."

"That sounds reasonable enough." I leaned my elbows onto the table, eyeing his notebook with curiosity. John's mind worked in a much more meandering and fanciful way than mine generally did, but over the years I'd come to value the unique contributions he could make from that perspective.

"I've started with the idea of visuals, just because we have to start somewhere." John turned a page in his journal to consult the notes he'd made there. A few rough sketches marked the space between them. "It shouldn't be too difficult to come up with the means to project patterns like Jemma's favorite Fibonacci sequence onto the outside of the building. Creating consistent visual stimuli *inside* will be harder, but we could bring smaller projectors and set them up in places the cultists aren't likely to stumble on them—or perhaps we could quickly have decals printed that we could stick to the walls?"

My thoughts had already turned to which of my nearest associates I might be able to call on to accomplish each of those things. "The decals would be more compact and more difficult to disrupt once in place. We'll simply need the patterns we want drawn up for the printing."

"I figured Jemma would want some input on that subject." John turned another page. "I started making some initial research into auditory stimuli, but that's a pretty complex area. I'll need more time. I thought I'd head back to the university library this afternoon—it's got a good collection."

"I suppose your medical expertise should be useful in this area," I said. "There are certain visual and auditory stimuli that had alter the mental states of regular human beings as well."

"There are. I was going to look into those too, although they'll depend somewhat on the individual people and their mental state. There isn't a catch-all beyond blaring sounds loud enough to be distracting or that sort of thing."

"Well, it's a start. Shall we see if we can get Jemma's thoughts on your initial ideas?"

"If she hasn't already charged off on her own despite our talk this morning," John muttered with a crooked smile.

From what I'd seen of Jemma's demeanor, I didn't think she'd have changed her mind again so quickly, but she was a difficult one to anticipate. Perhaps we really should get going.

We each grabbed one of the last two pastries, and John waved a waitress over to get the bill. As we walked back toward the hotel, John gazed around him, eagerly absorbing the sights of the city that as far as I knew he'd never visited before. It was something impressive about him that he could still take such delight in a relatively ordinary walk, even after the trials he'd been through in the military and beyond.

Another compulsion ran through me, even stronger

than before. I held myself back in a brief hesitation, but for fuck's sake, less than twenty-four hours ago I'd been as intimate with the man beside me as any two people could be. I knew he'd be pleased by the gesture. The only reason for me to balk was my own discomfort at shows of affection I'd generally thought of as facile.

But what was so facile, really, about making a concrete statement of what another person meant to you? John had to have been nervous making any gesture of that sort to me, but he'd put his feelings out there regardless.

I suppressed the flicker of nerves and reached out to take his hand.

Surprise flashed across John's face, but his fingers closed around mine in an instant. He didn't remark on the gesture, didn't even look at me, but I could sense the contentment that hummed off him all the same. *He* knew me well enough to understand that this one small action said more than any words I could have produced would have.

We were partners, yes, but more than that too. Much more than that, in ways that I still found somewhat inexplicable. But I had to admit my life felt fuller now than it had, even if I hadn't been aware I was missing anything until this unexpected flatmate had fallen into my lap.

We would face these literal demons and their sycophants together, and I would not let myself be shaken by uncertainty while this man stood by my side.

# CHAPTER FOURTEEN

*Jemma*

For some reason, I'd expected the elevator shaft to be cold. Maybe because the few times I'd found myself in one in the past, it'd been in much chillier climates.

The tall, ridged passage above me was gloomy, the maintenance lights on the top of the elevator car only providing a dull glow that reached partway up it, and the air had a slightly damp metallic smell. Still, I was already sweating from the heat in the enclosed space within a couple minutes of clambering through the panel I'd opened from inside the car. Obviously the air conditioning didn't penetrate the walls.

The surface beneath me vibrated as the car hummed upward on someone's command. I kept myself braced, watching the doorways slide by, ready to flatten myself to the roof if we appeared to be heading for the top floor. I wasn't sure exactly how much of a gap I'd get up there, but I'd rather not find out by slamming my head into the ceiling.

At the same time, I watched the video feed I'd patched into my phone from the tiny surveillance camera I'd added to the corner of the car. I wanted to see exactly how the building's inhabitants got access to the residential floors—and what those residents looked like.

They didn't venture out of their territory very often, I quickly gathered. In a normal apartment building, people would be coming and going all through the day. In the first hour of my surveillance, no passenger went any higher than the tenth floor of offices, and no one higher above summoned the car so they could come down. It was a good thing I'd worn the gold cuff that hid me from the shrouded folk's awareness, or any of the fiends hanging around here would have descended on me by now.

How long was I going to have to sit here to make my observations? And it wasn't only data I'd come to gather. My sister had managed to reach out to me across the divide between this world and the shrouded realm. If I got close enough to where they were keeping her in this building, assuming they had her captive here—if I could make her aware of my presence somehow—maybe we could communicate again.

Bash's drone photos had given us some sense of the interior layout on the upper floors. The first several above the tenth appeared to have kept to the blueprints with fairly standard apartment layouts, although in a few I'd been able to pick out tools of the cult's worship. They were definitely being used by a commune, if not the type I was used to.

The floors above those had mostly been hidden by curtains or shades, but the drone had managed to capture a little footage that showed large rooms with no dividing walls within view, markings on the floor—some of which looked like blood stains—and more of those tools scattered around. My best guess was that the cult members spent the more normal parts of their lives in the apartments and went up to the common areas above to conduct their more focused worship.

The very top few floors, we hadn't gotten even a peek at. I suspected if Olivia was being held in the building, it'd be up there. They might have an entire floor dedicated to keeping her captive and working whatever awful rituals they were using on her. Chances were it'd be the penthouse at the highest level, as close to our sun as the tower reached.

But I didn't know for sure, and as much as I wanted to scramble up the maintenance rungs and smash my way in there, I could recognize that the group plan I'd started to form with my men this morning gave me a better chance at seeing not just me but *her* out alive. Without any definite signs of where she was, I couldn't leap in with guns blazing or tossing explosives, or I'd be as likely to tear her apart as our enemies.

The elevator glided back down to the ground floor. I peered at my phone, and a smile crossed my lips as a middle-aged woman with gray-streaked hair got on. There was something about the hitch in her step—and yes, there it was. As the door slid closed, she swayed in a halting fashion to one side and the other: a cult motion of worship.

She slipped a keycard out of her tiny purse and pushed it into a slot on the control panel. While it was still inserted, she pressed the button for the fifteenth floor —one of the apartment levels. The elevator whirred upward, and she retrieved the card.

If the cultists left the building as infrequently as it

appeared, it'd be difficult to get our hands on one of those. Between Sherlock's and my connections, we could probably find someone reasonably local who could make a working facsimile, but only if the security system was generic enough. I wouldn't put it past the cult to have commissioned a custom system that a person would need direct access to in order to figure out the programming. We weren't likely to get away with that.

Of course, climbing the shaft was still a viable option.

And one I intended to make use of. I wasn't going to sit around all day hoping someone sent the elevator up to the top floors.

When the woman got off, I did too—grasping hold of the maintenance rungs and hefting myself upward. It only took a few heaves before I found my rhythm. Listening for any sound of the elevator rising after me, I clambered up the shaft one floor at a time.

The car dropped below me. Its lights dwindled in the distance. The vertical passage felt suddenly perilous, although I was sure of my grip. If I lost it, I wasn't going to survive the fall.

Climbing was definitely an option, but we'd need additional equipment if Sherlock with his cast or John with his weak leg were going to make it safely up the tower this way.

It was almost completely dark in the shaft by the time I reached the highest floors. I sensed more than saw the end of the passage above me. The heat had faded some as I'd climbed, but the effort had left my shirt sticking to my skin anyway.

I adjusted my position, looping one arm around the metal post that rose between the shallower rungs. With my feet steady on the rung beneath me and that arm solidly in place, I could relax enough to concentrate on things other than avoiding falling. I trained my attention on the wall in front of me and let the shadows wash through my mind.

"Olivia," I called in a low voice, as loud as I dared without risking that any regular person would hear me through the walls. Whatever the fiends had done to my sister, her awareness could slip across worlds. She'd been able to notice my presence near her before. I had to make myself as obvious to her as I could.

"Olivia. Olivia." I chanted her name over and over at intervals, like a sort of meditation. I was starting to feel a little hazy when a faint tingling sensation brushed over my face.

"Jemma?"

It was the same voice I'd heard in the shrouded realm, still with a faraway quality but not anywhere near as far as before. My heart skipped a beat.

"It's me, Olivia. I'm going to get you out of here. You're in the tower, aren't you?"

"Jemma… You shouldn't be here."

The mournfulness of her tone made me choke up. "Of course I should. I promised I'd come back for you, and I meant to do it years ago. I have friends. We can make it work. But it'll be easier the more I know about where exactly you are and how they're holding you."

"You don't know… Their plans are all wound through me. It's too tangled. As long as I'm here, they'll use me."

I leaned closer to the wall as if that would bring her to me, the ache in my throat running right down through my chest. If I could have just touched her, hugged her, shielded her the way I'd tried to so many times when we were kids…

"That's why I'm taking you away from here. We'll ruin their plans and take you someplace where you'll never have to deal with the bastards again. I swear it, Olivia. Do you know what floor you're on, even?"

Her voice took such a long time coming again that I started to think she wasn't going to answer. "High," she murmured. "So close to the sky. I can taste it through the roof."

She hadn't sounded that spacy even when she was ten. I hoped the effects of the shrouded folk's manipulations would fade once she was away from them. It sounded like she was on the top floor, as I'd suspected, at least.

"Are you near any windows?" I asked. "Do you see the elevator when people come up?" *Help me find you.*

Her voice was little more than a wisp now. "No windows. It's all dark. So dark when I open my eyes. The light is all inside. Sometimes it burns."

My hand tightened into a fist. If I could have punched every one of the fiends to Kingdom Come, I would have right this instant. My gaze traveled to the doorway across from me, meant to open for the elevator car. How crazy would it really be to force that open right now?

While all I had was my fists and the single pistol tucked in the back of my jeans? Pretty fucking crazy. The shrouded folk might not be able to see me while I wore the cuff around my thigh, but the cultists wouldn't have any trouble, and they were the ones with the semi-automatic rifles. There'd be plenty of them guarding this treasure their masters had preserved for so many years.

Gritting my teeth, I stayed in place. "I'll come for you as soon as I can," I said. "Do you know how soon the shrouded folk are hoping to complete their plans? Or what they're going to do in the city to add to their energy?"

If her inside knowledge could protect the people outside the tower too, I might as well find that out.

"I don't know. They want it all." A sound like a muted sob reached my ears, and my jaw clenched even harder. "Something's been gathering. It's all connected, here and there, inside me. Everything's tying together and pulling tight. The bridge is almost solid—days. It can't be more than days now." Her voice broke completely. "I don't want to help them. I want this to be over. I don't want them to use me like this."

"I know," I said fiercely. "I won't let them. I promise you that."

"Jemma…" All at once, her tone sharpened. "They're coming. They'll hear. I have to—don't let them find you. Please."

"Olivia!" I whispered.

She didn't respond. My stomach felt as if it'd twisted into one huge knot. I leaned my forehead against the cool metal pole and fought back a scream of frustration.

All the horrors and all the pain they'd put her through, and she was worried about them hurting *me*.

The shrouded folk were close to their goal. Just days away, from what she could feel. That matched the urgency I'd sensed. It was better than hours, anyway.

She was waiting for me. I'd made a promise back then, and I'd made it again—I wouldn't let the fiends take her. And that meant we'd better get on with figuring out how to end the shrouded folk for good.

Dragging in a breath, I shifted my position to begin the long climb down to the bottom of the shaft.

*Jemma*

"Well, I'm pretty sure that fellow thinks I've gone barmy," John said as he hung up the phone.

I glanced up from my laptop where I'd been working at making my own arrangements on his suite's sofa. All of us had gotten down to work at gathering whatever necessary equipment we could lay our hands on after our most recent strategy discussion.

"He didn't think requisitioning a bunch of high tech medical equipment in a rush for a supposed police operation was a normal request?" I said wryly.

"Not particularly." John rubbed his forehead. "He may still come through. Or our other options for getting the right kind of auditory effect may turn out to be equally effective." He looked to Sherlock, across the table from him. "Have your contacts offered much so far?"

"I've begun with the visual side of things," the detective said. "I believe I should be able to come up with projectors and mounts that will cover at least the majority of the tower's exterior. It is rather a tall order, though. I've gotten some bemused comments."

I took a sip from my coffee as I studied the two of them, letting the sugar-laced bitterness soothe a momentary twinge of anxiety. "It's going to be something of a spectacle when it all comes together. This isn't going to be a peaceful raid. Are you sure you're not getting yourselves into more trouble than you'll be able to get out of, calling in all these favors?"

Not that I wanted to turn away their help—I might have been able to get my hands on just as much equipment alone, but it'd have taken a hell of a lot more time. I was merely highly conscious of the fact that most of my and Bash's arrangements in the last couple hours had involved items designed for slaughter.

I wanted to see my men, my sister, and me out of that building alive, yes, but every other person residing in it could meet their maker as far as I was concerned. If no one was left alive, then there'd be no one to make another stab at carrying out the shrouded folk's warped plans.

"Let us worry about how to handle the authorities on our side of the law," Sherlock said, his voice dry. Then he went back to frowning at the diagram he'd been studying.

They were grown men. They could look after themselves, make their own decisions. I'd been up against the shrouded folk on my own for so long, not even telling Bash the real reasons behind the connections and wealth I'd accumulated, that it was still hard to let go of the sense that the fiends were my responsibility and no one else's. Especially when I'd seen so much more of their horrors than anyone else here had.

A text popped up on my phone from Bash, who'd been making his inquiries in person. *Supplier agreed to make a deal for most of what was on your list. Hand-off scheduled for five, outside the city. I'll just need the money.*

*Of course,* I wrote back. *Why most and not all? Did you tell him we'll double the price to get things shipped across borders?*

*This has all been through a middleman so far, but I got the impression he's leery about the size of the order. I think he's coming to the hand-off personally.*

As if it was any of the black-market businessman's concern how much I bought from him, as long as I paid. I grimaced at the phone in momentary hesitation and then wrote, *I should come too then, just to make sure it all goes smoothly. Where should I meet you?*

For the last few years, I'd let Bash handle almost all of my face-to-face transactions. The type of people I dealt with on *my* side of the law tended to respect a brawny ex-sniper a hell of a lot more than a skinny young woman who didn't look like she could snap them in half—even though I could. But if this asshole was going to give even Bash a hard time, maybe he needed a reminder of who exactly he was dealing with. I'd be happy to give him a demonstration.

Bash knew better than to argue the idea. He just texted me a spot at the north end of town. I took a little more time in the suite to arrange the cash I'd need, which I could pick up on the way, and then got up.

"I should have most of my part of the inventory covered. Off to collect it with Bash now."

John gave me a playful salute on my way out. I stopped in my own room to drop off my laptop and arm myself with a pistol and a knife. As I stepped back into the hall, Garrett was just coming down it toward Sherlock and John's suite.

He slowed when he saw me, and I paused, feeling unreasonably awkward. We hadn't talked one-on-one since he'd showed up out of the blue this morning. I had the sense the conversations we'd had since that moment on the mountain weren't exactly finished, but I wasn't sure how to resolve them.

"Heading out?" he said, in a casual tone as if nothing all that momentous was going on, but his gaze was serious as he waited for my response.

"Making sure the crooks I have to deal with don't screw us over," I said with a small smile. "Are you only just getting back from the detention center?"

"Yes. Unfortunately the cult members here are as tight-lipped as anywhere else. I could tell they didn't like the fact that I was poking at the possibility of there being more destructive plans in the works, but I can't say I have any better idea what those plans might be." He let out a breath. "I guess my next job will be making sure the local police don't interfere with *our* plans. Can I assume these 'crooks' you're seeing won't be directly involved in those?"

"It's just the five of us who'll be seeing things through," I said. "So, only the crooks you already know."

The joke fell flat with the tightening of Garrett's mouth. The sight made my innards tighten in turn.

"I don't really have time to talk right now," I added. "But perhaps we should, when we both have a moment, just the two of us? To clear the air?"

His expression relaxed a little. "I think that would be good. But Jemma?"

"Yes?"

He moved closer to me, with that electric intensity none of my other men could quite match. His hand came up to touch my cheek. "I don't look at you and see a crook," he said quietly, and tipped his head to bring his lips to mine.

When he kissed me like that, like he'd never wanted anyone more, I wished I didn't have some idiot supplier I needed to deal with. I'd much rather have given all my attention over to the man who was giving me his forgiveness with the heat of his mouth and the caress of his fingertips over my skin. I leaned into him for a moment, but he would still be here when I got back, and the supplies might not be if I didn't make sure of it. Reluctantly, I drew back.

"We'll definitely have to have that conversation—soon," I said, and a smile flitted across his face in answer.

By the time I reached Bash's meeting spot, I had a car with a locked case full of cash and a film of dust coating my throat. As I ditched the car and carried the case over to the delivery truck Bash had gotten his hands on, I gulped from a bottle of lemonade I'd picked up. The sour sweetness only left my mouth sticky.

"I'm not looking forward to this," I muttered as I got in. Navigating city streets on four wheels rarely put me in a good mood.

"I can still do the hand-off myself," Bash offered.

"No. Part of the reason I'm not looking forward to it is I have a feeling there'll be some kind of trouble."

We left the dense urban sprawl behind quickly, heading farther north past shabby-looking warehouses behind even shabbier concrete walls and patches of sparse forestland. "Do you think we have anything major to worry about from this guy?" I asked Bash.

"His people didn't seem hostile. There was just a lot of back and forth working out the deal, and he definitely balked over a few requests." Bash shrugged. "Who knows what's gotten into him. Maybe the blast downtown yesterday has him jumpy, even though it should be obvious we didn't have anything to do with that."

"We've been investing in his operations for a while. I really can't see how I've given him anything to complain about—or any reason to think we won't make good on any arrangements we make."

"Of course you haven't, Majesty," Bash said affectionately. "And if he isn't a total moron, he'll be there with the goods when he said he'd be, and you won't even need to get out of the truck. You've been good to people, and most of them know what's happened to the idiots who didn't appreciate that."

His confidence didn't completely reassure me. Even John's and Sherlock's contacts were giving them some grief over this operation, and I didn't exactly have the same kind of rapport with my business connections.

Bash pulled into the yard of one of the more distant warehouses. Around the back of the aluminum-sided building, a couple of guys were waiting by a truck of their own. One of them held up his hand, partly in greeting and partly to motion for us to park about a dozen feet back. A prickle ran down my spine. They were treating us like uncertain associates rather than long-established allies.

Bash hopped out, leaving the case with the money with me. An older guy got out of the other truck and sauntered to meet him in the middle of the yard. His gaze twitched to me behind the windshield and then back to my right-hand man. I rested my arm in the open window, watching and listening intently.

"Do you have all the items we agreed on?" Bash asked with a jerk of his chin toward the truck.

"I was able to get it all together, pretty impressive

given the time window you gave me." The guy folded his sinewy arms over his chest. "What are you going to do with all that shit anyway? You starting a war or something?"

Ending it was more like it. I restrained a smile.

Bash glowered at the man. "I don't see how that matters. We need the equipment. We're paying you for it. The rest is our business, not yours."

"I just want to be sure there isn't going to be some big blow-up that comes back to haunt me. You've got to understand, as one businessman to another."

"We keep our books clean. You don't need to worry about anyone connecting you to anything."

The guy swiped his hand over his ratty beard. "All the same, I think I need a little insurance, considering the extreme nature of this deal. You want the full load? I'm going to need double the payment we talked about before."

The fucker. We were already paying a hell of a lot more than the stuff would have cost him to get to make up for the short notice.

"We've brought what we agreed on," Bash said. "That's what you're getting."

"I can wait while you get together the rest. Or you can leave with just half the stuff. It's up to you."

Before he'd even finished that last sentence, I pushed open the truck door. The guy stiffened as I strode across the concrete with sharp raps of my shoes.

"Teppo, isn't it?" I said, coming to a stop beside Bash. "You know who I am. You know you wouldn't have your fingers in half as many pies as you've managed without my assistance. So what's all this bullshit now? When have I given you any indication I'd screw you over?"

His eyes went twitchy again. "I— You've got to see— It's not about screwing over. I've never delivered a load like this to anyone. I don't even know what you'd do with some of the stuff in there. And if you're doing to do something crazy, then I've got to cover my ass."

"Watch how you talk to her," Bash said in a growl, taking a menacing step forward.

I caught his elbow to hold him back and gave Teppo a thin smile. "*I've* been covering *your* ass for the last four years, making sure you have a leg up over competitors, settling disputes in your favor, only asking a very small portion of your earnings as payment. I don't believe I've let you down once. And the thanks I get is the suggestion that *I'm* going to be bad for your business? I'll give you one more chance to reconsider your stance. The money is in the truck."

The guy's mouth opened and closed a few times like a fish drowning in air. Finally he mumbled, "Look, I've got to do what's best for me, and I need that extra cash to make this right."

The emotion that came over me wasn't even anger. It was simply resignation shot through with a dollop of irritation.

I didn't need this guy anymore. All the plans I'd been building up to were culminating within the week, and then… if I survived… I wasn't even sure how far I'd keep up the business. So if he wanted to be a jackass about it, let him find out what jackasses got.

"I think you've forgotten who you're dealing with, Teppo," I said, low and clear. "The only person here acting crazy and fucking up your business is *you*. To make sure you remember what kind of respect is due in future, I'm imposing an asshole tax on this transaction. Everything in that truck is mine, and I'll keep the cash too, thank you very much."

Teppo's eyes widened. One of his men reached for a gun at his side, but Bash was faster. He had his pistol in hand in an instant, aimed at Teppo's head.

"Try it, and say goodbye to your boss," he said.

"Now, just wait a—" Teppo said, starting to sputter.

I cut him off with a wave of my own pistol. "Keys. Now."

"There's no way I—"

I shot the ground, so close to his foot that smoke wisped from the toe of his shoe. "Keys." When he simply stared at me, I shot again, this time aiming for the side of his calf.

The bullet tore through his cargo pants and flesh with a spray of blood. Teppo cried out and crumpled onto his ass, clutching at his leg. I walked up to him, gun still at the ready.

"Keys," I said. "Or I'm going to keep working my way up. And believe me, the damage will quickly become permanent."

Teppo made an anguished jerk of his hand toward one of his underlings. The younger guy, his face tensed, fished out a car key and tossed it to me. I pitched it to Bash, who caught it without his gun wavering even half an inch.

"We're not going to leave you stuck out here in the middle of nowhere," I said, heading back to our truck. I grabbed the case with the money and left the doors open. "Get your boss to a hospital before he loses more blood than he needs to. And don't mess with me again unless you want to see how much worse the consequences can get."

Bash and I circled the three men on opposite sides.

One of the underlings had wrenched off his shirt to press it to his boss's wound. The other scrambled to the truck. Bash threw the key after him with a clink as it hit the pavement.

The punishment had been brutal, efficient… and I wasn't enjoying the moment at all. From the cab of Teppo's truck, I peered down at the limping man and the splotches of blood marking the concrete, and weariness swept through me.

I was bored of these clashes, the power plays, the asserting of dominance. More than ten years of it, all to climb high enough to challenge the shrouded folk, and I was ready to step back from all this crap. If I ever got the chance to make that choice.

# CHAPTER SIXTEEN

*John*

The pile of books on my "finished" side was finally higher than on my "to read" side, but I still didn't feel as if I'd made a lot of headway. I made a face at the text I was currently skimming through, the author of which kept hedging his suggestions with uncertain language about how most of his propositions were only theoretical. The rasp as I flipped the page sounded loud in the quiet of the university library.

A rustle of fabric approached my table. I glanced up, and my pulse skipped a beat with a mix of happiness and guilt. Happiness because Jemma's form sinking into the chair across from me was a welcome and unexpected sight, and guilt because I'd meant to have more to tell her when I did see her again.

She was carrying a plastic bag, which also rustled. With a sly grin, she slid it across the table toward me.

"Still buried in the books, I see. Sherlock told me you'd probably still be here. It's past seven, you know. I'm going to guess you haven't had any dinner yet." She nodded to the bag, which was giving off a spicy, meaty smell that had already set my mouth watering. "I picked you up some kofta kabobs from that restaurant you liked so much the first night."

"You figured I needed looking after, did you?" I said, but she wasn't wrong. My stomach gurgled at the smell. I looked at my current book and pushed it to the side. "I don't think eating's allowed in here."

"Afraid to break the rules now?" Jemma teased with a glint in her lovely gray eyes, but she got up at the same time. "I'm sure we can find a good enough spot somewhere on campus. Whatever you're mulling over, taking a break from the books will probably help the ideas come together anyway. And even if it doesn't, we can't have our doctor starving himself to death."

"I'm not exactly a medical practitioner anymore," I couldn't help pointing out, but I got up, taking the bag of food and my journal full of notes with me.

We ended up sitting on the grass beneath the campus's huge stone gate with its impressive arches. Jemma, naturally, had picked up a pastry full of custard for herself. She nibbled at it, appearing it savor each bite, while I worked through the kababs. As I polished off the last one, she licked the sugar and flecks of cream from her fingers with flashes of tongue that stirred a different sort of hunger in me. Then she sat back on her hands and gave me a pointed look.

"All right. Let's hear what you've come up with. I want the chance to try out the strategies we're considering using ahead of time, so we've got to get moving with any more equipment we need to gather."

I nodded. The texts had repeated the same themes

enough that I didn't even need to consult my notes to go over the general concepts.

"Sounds, especially loud and unexpected ones, can have an adverse effect on heart rate and blood pressure," I said. "Continual noise elevates cortisol levels, which results in fatigue, irritability, difficulty concentrating, and sometimes more acute physical symptoms like headaches. Those are the most definite effects we could count on. If we can work a pattern in while also making the sound disruptive, I assume we'd be interfering with both your fiends' and the cultists' ability to fight back."

"So we want an irritating rhythm," Jemma said with obvious amusement. "I think we can manage that."

"Another factor is actual talking," I said. "Bash mentioned that he helped keep the shrouded folk away in Tokyo by playing Shakespearean movies—he figured something about the rhythm to the dialogue repelled them. There's also been research suggesting that hearing conversations going on around you hinders mental processes like short-term memory, which makes it harder to complete tasks."

The corner of Jemma' mouth quirked upward. "Tasks like 'Let's tackle these intruders who've just broken in'? I don't see why we couldn't give that a try too. Was there anything else?"

I shook my head, a pang of my earlier guilt returning. "Those are the connections that've been researched the most and shown consistency. I'm not sure how much we'd want to gamble. I was going to keep looking, though. And I've taken notes on specific kinds of sounds that showed the most detrimental effects, that sort of thing."

"I'm not sure we'll need more than that." Jemma exhaled slowly, her gaze going distant for a moment. The sinking sun was casting the sky overhead with a rosy hue only a little less vibrant than her hair. "I suppose the difficult part is going to be finding equipment that will effectively conduct the sound through walls and so on, and getting it all up to the higher floors of that building without them noticing. Maybe if we could set up some things outside, by the windows… I'll have to look into the sound conductivity of glass."

"You might ask Sherlock. I'd say there's a fifty percent chance that's one of the many subjects he's decided he needed to investigate for one reason or another in the past."

Jemma gave a short laugh. "He is something of a repository of knowledge, isn't he? I'll start there. It'd certainly be easier if he's done the work for us ahead of time."

I chuckled. "Well, easy depends on how much you enjoy listening to him pontificate rather than consulting the books for yourself."

"Yes." She lay back on the grassy slope, tucking her hands behind her head and considering the streaks of cloud that crossed the sky. Then she shifted her gaze to me. "You enjoy his pontificating."

It was a statement rather than a question, but she said it mildly, without any sign of where she was going with the observation.

"I'll be the first to admit he can go on too long," I said. "But the energy that comes over him when he latches on to a subject—it really is something to see."

"It is." She was silent for a minute or so, long enough that I started to wonder if she expected me to take my leave, and then she said, softly but succinctly, "Are you sure you wouldn't be happier with just him?"

I blinked. "What do you mean?"

She arched her eyebrows at me. "I mean… you all went to a lot of trouble to convince me to stick around, painted a picture of this future where we'll all keep on having whatever exactly relationship we have right now. That's no surprise coming from Bash, and I could see Garrett wanting that too, but you and Sherlock have each other. Doesn't adding me to the mix just overly complicate things?"

I hesitated, at a loss for words as I tried to sort through the feelings her words had stirred to the surface. There was a quiver of excitement, yes, at the thought that Sherlock and I had anything that could really be called a relationship. But the way Jemma seemed to think she could be so easily cut from that dynamic made my chest clench.

She was brilliant, no doubt about it, and those glinting gray eyes saw a lot. They clearly didn't see everything, though. Somehow she'd missed the way I looked at her, the way every part of me responded to her. Somehow she couldn't see how right now just taking her in, from the waves of her scarlet hair against the green of the grass to the creamy paleness of her skin, the narrow lips I'd come to know the shape and taste of so well, the slender curves of her sprawled body that contained so much condensed strength… It kindled not just a fire in my loins but a heady warmth that filled my heart.

This beautiful, brilliant, complicated woman had crashed into our lives with startling grace and care, had twisted us around her finger and yet woken us up at the same time. I wouldn't have Sherlock the way I did now at all if it wasn't for her. I probably still wouldn't have admitted to myself what mattered to me.

And one of the things that mattered to me was her.

"I'd have thought you knew me well enough by now to realize that complications are a feature, not a defect, as far as I'm concerned," I said with a crooked smile. "I like a little trouble along the way. That's what makes it fun."

She rolled her eyes at me. "There's trouble and then there's 'likely to get you killed in half a dozen ways in any given month'."

"I don't see how that'll be much of a concern once we've dealt with these monsters. Unless you're planning on bringing violent criminal associates around to our doorstep."

She grimaced. "No. I'd rather not have them even at my doorstep."

"Then what's the problem?" I asked.

"I just don't want you to feel some sort of obligation because of what we've been through and what we've shared, if your heart's more elsewhere already. I won't be offended. I'm *glad* the two of you have each other the way you do."

"Jemma…" My throat tightened with emotion. "Do I really need to tell you that you mean more to me than that? I can't imagine living my life without Sherlock in it, no, but it'd seem awfully drab without you in it too."

"You managed fine for years without me in it."

"I managed without being more than Sherlock's completely platonic colleague too." I let out an exasperated huff. "You spark something in me no one else does, not even him. Something I don't want to lose. I'm head-over-heels in love with you, Jemma. Has it really not been obvious?"

She stared at me for a second. Then she pushed herself back into a sitting position, her gaze never leaving my face. "No. Not—I mean—it's not an area I have a lot of experience in."

Her startled uncertainty brought an even sharper warmth into my chest. She knew how to tackle everything except tenderness, didn't she? "I forgave you for pushing my best friend down a cliff. I've followed you everywhere you've let me follow." I paused. "Maybe I can't offer Sherlock's genius or Garrett's fervor or whatever else, maybe I can't make the most impressive confession ever, but—"

"John," she said, cutting me off. She set her hand over mine and squeezed, her eyes searching my face, and for the first time I noticed the sort of desperation that colored them, as if she were both afraid of what she might see and afraid she wouldn't see it at all. "You're wonderful the way you are. I think you're what keeps the rest of us from falling apart. Don't ever, *ever* suggest you're somehow worth less than anyone else."

"I could say the same right back to you," I said quietly.

She went still. "Yes. Well." Then she leaned in and brushed her lips to mine so quickly I barely had time to react.

"Thank you," she murmured by my ear. I caught her before she could pull back and hugged her to me. She leaned her head against my shoulder, and for one fleeting moment I felt her relax against me, like all the weight in the world had lifted off of her.

The business side of her took over before long. "You'd better get back to those books if you're going to finish before the library closes," she said, but her tone had a gentleness to it that hadn't been there before.

"Very true," I said, getting to my feet.

She gave me a peck on my cheek and a squeeze of my arm before she loped away. It occurred to me as I watched her disappear into the dwindling evening light that I wasn't completely sure what she'd been thanking me for. That was all right, though. It was enough that I'd said something she'd thought it worth thanking me for at all.

One more offering that might hold her back from throwing her whole life on the pyre to make the shrouded folk burn.

# CHAPTER SEVENTEEN

*Jemma*

W hen Garrett answered my knock on his hotel room door, he looked as if he'd already started to turn in for the night. He'd unbuttoned his light blue dress shirt halfway down his chest, and his hair was more rumpled than usual, in a rather appealing way.

"Is this a good time for our talk?" I asked with a cock of my head.

He ran his hand over his hair a little self-consciously, but he stepped back to let me in. One of the pillows on his bed was propped upright with his ever-present notepad lying on the covers beside it—he must have been relaxing there while he went over the case.

I nodded to the notepad. "Any new developments since this afternoon?"

"A good one, actually," Garrett said, his usual energy coming back to him as he shut the door behind me. "The local police have agreed to monitor the comings and goings from the tower and to tail anyone who shows indications of being a cultist. Right now, there's an officer watching a small group that left about an hour ago. All they've done is get dinner so far, but if they start preparing to cause any trouble, someone should be able to intervene."

That was a welcome development—although it depended on the police's ability to ID the actual cultists. If the commune noticed the surveillance, they'd be more careful about their behavior leaving the building.

"I suppose getting bugs planted inside the apartments would be too much to ask," I said.

"If we could draw a definite connection between crimes already committed and the inhabitants, maybe not, but even in that case, it'd still take more time than it sounds like we have."

"Yeah." I sank down on the end of the bed, all the events of the day from the "intervention" to talking with John at the library pressing down on me with a sudden weight. We'd accomplished so much in just one day… but there was still so much we'd need to do before we could destroy those fucking fiends, or at least their connection to our world.

I didn't want to think about what would happen if we weren't fast enough.

Garrett sat down next to me, close enough to be companionable without being overly familiar. As if we could get any more familiar than we'd already been. But we hadn't really talked, hadn't touched more than that kiss in the hall, since I'd nearly destroyed any trust I'd gained from my trio of detectives, and his tentativeness sent a twinge through me.

How much was he being respectful of my space and how much was he asserting his own need?

It should be easy enough to tell. I slid my hand across the bedspread toward his, waiting for his reaction. Without hesitation, he met me halfway and grasped my fingers with his.

All right, then. The space was for my benefit. He was looking out for me like he had been this morning, like he'd been by coming here at all.

I couldn't leave it alone, though. Poking at the subject felt like picking at a scab, but the fact was, a wound like this couldn't really heal if we just ignored it. If I tried to pretend nothing had ever been amiss, it'd only fester in both of us. Better to drain any lingering poison out of it now.

"You couldn't have been feeling this forgiving right after I gave Sherlock that shove."

"No, I'd say that's an understatement." He let out a rough laugh under his breath. "I was furious. And hurt. I should admit that too."

"Because you expected better of me."

His hand stayed clasped around mine. "Because I didn't know the full story, and in the moment it looked as if you really meant to kill him, and…"

"And?" I prompted him when he trailed off.

"Honestly, because it reminded me of the worst parts of myself."

I gave him a quizzical look, and he offered me a sheepish smile in return before lowering his gaze.

"I've told you about all the anger that drove my behavior when I was a child, out of jealousy and frustration. You caught me struggling with the urge to slash my colleague's bloody tires not that long ago. If anyone should know anything about tackling problems with unnecessary violence, it's me."

"You didn't slash those tires," I pointed out. "You'd already gotten a hold on yourself before you even realized I was there."

"And you didn't really try to kill Sherlock," Garrett replied. "You were trying to go off on your own like you've done before, and he'd proven how dogged he'd be about following you… and you had your sister's life and freedom to consider. Hell, for all we know, we'd have met a worse fate than a tumble if we'd come charging right after you."

My throat tightened. "You still might."

"You see?" He lifted my hand to rest it against his thigh and raised his head to meet my eyes again. "*That* is who you are. Who you've shown yourself to be with every honest gesture and comment you've offered the entire time I've known you. None of this has ever been for *you*, especially once you ended that deal. You could have lived the rest of your life without giving the demons a second thought. You could have thrown us into the fray ahead of you. But every step of the way, you've been fighting to stop them from hurting more people the way they hurt you and your sister, you've been trying to leave us out of it so we won't get hurt too…"

"I'm not a martyr," I protested.

"No. I'm not saying you are. But in spite of being a criminal mastermind, you're still one of the most selfless people I've ever met. When this is over, when we kick them off the face of this Earth and get your sister out of their clutches, then are you finally going to let yourself have a few things that are just for you?"

Staring back into his dark brown eyes, I couldn't say I completely agreed. "I've indulged myself now and then. If

I were really so selfless, I'd have gone and stormed the tower by myself no matter what the bunch of you said."

Garrett raised an eyebrow. "Why didn't you, then?"

"Because I want this more than I probably should."

I leaned in, and he met my kiss, his mouth hot and tender all at once. No, I wasn't selfless when it came to these men. I was fucking greedy. Deep down, I wanted all of them, everything they'd give me, even the parts I couldn't give in return.

Garrett slid his free hand along the side of my neck, brushing my hair back over my shoulder. He cupped my jaw and kissed me again at an even better angle. The soft but eager press of his lips set off that familiar flame running down through my chest to smolder low in my belly. I ran my fingers up his chest to the open V of his collar to trace the lean muscles there.

He pulled back an inch, resting his forehead against mine, his breath ragged. "I missed you, firecracker," he said. "Even when I was furious with you, I missed you."

My pulse stuttered with an emotion that was both hopeful and pained. But I could return that sentiment.

"I missed you too," I said softly.

"Even with Sherlock and the rest around to keep you occupied?"

"The group doesn't feel complete without you there." I paused. "I don't feel complete. There are ways we understand each other that I don't have with anyone else." That was true for each of the guys, really. So perhaps I couldn't be blamed for wanting to keep all of them by my side.

It must have been the right thing to say, because Garrett kissed me even harder, his arm looping around my waist to pull me right up against his wiry frame. I eased one leg across his lap, half straddling him, so we could fit even more tightly together, and a groan caught in his throat. He smelled as delicious as he always did, like a flare of electricity, smoky and potent. Irresistible. How could I not devour this man?

But some small fragment of me wasn't entirely satisfied by the forgiveness and affection he'd already expressed. That selfish particle of longing that held me back for a second even as I unbuttoned the rest of his shirt.

The request slipped out. "Say it again?"

Garrett had just tugged my blouse free from my skirt. He stopped with his hand on my bare skin below my breast and peered at me searchingly. "It?"

An embarrassed warmth crept through my chest, but that didn't prevent me from continuing. "What you told me, that day with Bash. If it's still true. I know I can't say it back, but I—I think I'd like hearing it."

For a second, I felt ridiculously awkward, like a schoolgirl confessing her first crush. What was wrong with me? But any regret that'd come over me at asking washed away with Garrett's softly beaming smile.

"I love you," he said, tipping his head so close his lips brushed mine a hair's breadth from another kiss. They teased across my cheek toward my ear. "I love you, Jemma."

I *couldn't* say the words back. Even as my heart swelled with affection for this man, too much of it was devoted to my sister and the cause I'd spent my whole life working toward. But I could show him a sort of love I expected he'd very much enjoy.

I nudged him higher on the bed as I peeled off his shirt. He tugged off my blouse in turn. While he eased down the straps of my bra, his mouth branding my collarbone with a blissful heat, I opened the fly of his slacks. I curled my fingers around his already rigid cock and was rewarded with the hitch of his breath.

"Jemma," he murmured, all hunger now. I slipped from his grasp and sank over his hips with a swipe of my tongue over the head of his cock. His voice turned choked. "Fucking bloody hell."

"I'll translate that as, 'Please do go on'," I teased, and took him right into my mouth.

His only response was an inarticulate sound. He slumped back on the bed, but he kept one hand on my shoulder with a continuous caress, growing shakier as I swirled my tongue around his velvety flesh. I hadn't attended to Garrett like this before. His cock tasted like the rest of him, only sharper, as if I was drawing a live current into me with the movements of my lips.

I was never going to be a normal girlfriend. I'd never be made of sweetness and light. But I could damn well give it good in some respects. I didn't think any of my men would look back on our time together with disappointment, however things worked out in the end.

Garrett's hips jerked as I sucked him down harder. A groan escaped his lips. He gripped my shoulder harder and then pulled at me to stop. When I raised my head, he urged me up the bed beside him, rolling onto me when our bodies aligned. The feel of his weight pressing down on me sent a fresh wave of desire through me from head to toe.

"We haven't done it in a bed yet," he said, kissing my cheek and then my jaw. "This will be an interesting experiment. If you don't think it's too outrageous."

I laughed, squirming so his erection would come to

rest against just the right spot between my legs. It was true, we'd made use of desks and dressers and rugs but never an actual bed in the past. "I think I can handle this," I said, and gasped as his cock slid against me.

He fumbled along my hip for my skirt's zipper, and together we peeled it off of me. A growl of frustration slipped out of me when I realized my purse wasn't in reach. Garrett let out a soft chuckle.

"Call me optimistic, but I came prepared," he murmured, and reached to grab a packet out of the bedside table's drawer.

He paused before opening it to dip his head to my breasts, lavishing them with the attention he hadn't gotten the chance to offer earlier. My fingers curled into his hair as he flicked his tongue over my nipple with a flare of pleasure. For a second, I was torn between lingering in that bliss and careening onward to the greater ecstasy ahead. Then I pulled him back up to claim his mouth—or maybe he was claiming mine—it didn't really matter when his cock was penetrating me a few moments later.

I arched upward so he could plunge in all the way to the hilt. Garrett gripped my thigh and bowed his head. As he plowed into me hard and fast, he nipped my shoulder with a smaller spark of pleasure.

It wasn't the most outrageous sex I'd ever had by a longshot, not even in the past week, but the desire in his touch and the urgency of his thrusts brought a different sort of high. We were in sync, in more ways than one—in ways I'd never have thought I could connect with a man so devoted to justice and the law.

I crossed my ankles behind him and cried out as he hit the most sensitive spot deep inside me. My head lolled back with the rush of my coming release. Garrett clutched me to him, keeping his strokes firm and fast, the intensity of his lust as giddying as the ecstatic burn of him filling me.

I came just seconds before he did, with another cry and a quiver that ran through every inch of me, flooding me with bliss.

Garrett eased me down on the mattress, but he stayed braced over me, gazing down at me. I gave him a pleased smile in return. He'd better be able to tell just how much *I'd* enjoyed that. But something else, something slightly nervous, darted through his gaze.

"It's a big bed," he said cautiously. "I wouldn't mind sharing it for the night. And then you'd be right on hand if the police have any updates for me."

Oh, this dear, lovely man. Emotion caught in my throat, recognizing what the invitation meant to him and how uncertain he was of how I'd receive it. The truth was that a few months ago, maybe even a few weeks ago, the thought would have made me edgy. Now it only melted me even more.

I could do this much. I could let myself have this much. Hell, it might be my last chance.

"In that case," I said, "I'm not going anywhere."

# CHAPTER EIGHTEEN

*Jemma*

I was meandering through a dreamland Istanbul, streets merging with one another, a single turn taking me from the middle of one neighborhood to a totally separate one, when a voice drifted to me as if carried on a faint breeze.

"Jemma," it whispered. "Jemma, can you hear me?"

I spun around outside a temple and found myself by the shop where I'd picked up last night's dessert. The voice came again—from a different direction? Or from all around and yet whisper-soft at the same time.

"Are you there, Jemma?"

It was Olivia's voice. The recognition shot through me with a jolt of adrenaline—and I jerked awake in Garrett's bed, sweat forming on my skin and heart thudding.

Garrett stirred at my sharp inhalation, reaching to touch my side from where he was sprawled under the covers beside me. "Okay?" he mumbled, still half asleep.

"I—I don't know. I have to..." My thoughts were

muddled. I shook my head and burrowed it back into the pillow. As I closed my eyes, I strained my ears, but my sister's voice didn't reach me again.

She hadn't projected it to me physically. She'd touched my mind somehow—some way she only could when I was in that in-between world of dreams?

I willed my breath to even out and tried to let my mind drift back into slumber. Unfortunately, my senses were far too much on high alert now. My muscles wouldn't quite relax; my thoughts spun restlessly in my head. After a few minutes that only made me more tense than I'd been to start with, I pushed out of the bed.

Garrett woke up more as I padded across the room, pulling my clothes back on in the hint of dawn light that was just starting to seep past the curtain. He squinted at the clock, which read 5:47, and then at me. "Jemma, what's wrong?"

"I think my sister was trying to tell me something while I was sleeping. So I have to get back to sleep. And it's not happening on its own."

He heaved off the covers and grabbed the thin hotel bathrobe. "Are you sure you weren't just dreaming?"

No. But… "It didn't feel like part of my dream. It felt like when I talked to her in the shrouded realm." I grasped the door handle. "I need to talk to Bash."

There wasn't much Garrett could contribute to the situation, but I didn't argue about him following me either. Because he'd come to Istanbul later than the rest of us, he'd ended up on the same floor but at the other end of the hall. I slipped past the closed doors where other patrons were sleeping and knocked as loud as I dared on Bash's.

The hitman never slept all that deeply. He was at the

door within a matter of seconds, peering at me a little blearily but more alert than Garrett still looked. His gaze slid past me to the other man, but if he had any qualms left about the fact that he was sharing my affections with other lovers, it didn't show in his expression.

"What's going on? What do you need?" he asked.

I motioned him back into his room, and Garrett and I joined him there. I glanced around the darkened space. "Do you still have the leftover pills from the ritual we did in Tokyo?"

"I wasn't sure if you'd want to pass over again," he said, frowning. "They're in my suitcase. Are you going back right now?"

"No, not exactly. I just need to get back into a state like sleep. I'll take half a dose."

"She thinks her sister was trying to talk to her in a dream," Garrett offered by way of explanation.

Bash nodded as if that were an everyday occurrence and fished the pill bottle out of one of the hidden compartments in his suitcase. I poured one of the tiny pills onto my hand, eyeballed it, and managed to crack it almost perfectly in two with a jerk of my thumbs. One half, I popped into my mouth and swallowed with just saliva.

I might not have been thinking as straight as usual with my early waking and my impatience to get back to my sister. "You should lie down," Garrett reminded me.

I headed toward Bash's bed, and the medication's effects rippled through me. My balance wobbled. The men caught me and helped me the last few steps. I slumped down on one side of the mattress with the vague thought that I needed to leave room there for the two of them, they might want to get more sleep too, and then my mind tumbled away from me into a shifting haze.

A vague awareness of the room and people around me lingered, but I couldn't have tracked their movements or spoken to them if I'd wanted to. My consciousness drifted deeper into the haze, on a plane somewhere between meditation and sleep. *Olivia*, I thought, but I didn't know how to speak to her across the distance the way she'd spoken to me.

I didn't need to. She was waiting for me. The haze solidified around me into vague shapes of buildings and streets, and that faint whisper tickled my ears again. "Jemma. You came back."

"I'll always come back," I said. "How did you—no, it doesn't matter. What did you need to tell me?"

"They're doing something," my sister said. "They're—I can feel the energy rising—I can feel—"

"What?" I said, my stomach knotting.

For a few seconds, she was silent. Then a sensation brushed over my arm, delicate as a moth's wing, and a set of impressions that weren't mine trickled through my body.

Little electric jolts twitched through my nerves. There was a vast dark space and a sprawl of gray land that I recognized as the shrouded realm. Mixed between those came hints of moving traffic and sunlight reflecting off of windows—fragments of the city around us.

All of it flowed through me as it must have been flowing through Olivia, as if she were all those places at the same time or connected to beings who were. With a distant slash of a knife and welling of blood came a sharper flash of energy. It twined all through her being, winding around her throat, creeping across her lungs, penetrating her gut. The ruddy glow of it set my nerves jittering the way the light in the shrouded folk's stones had.

They'd tied her up in their schemes in a totally literal way. Their essence ran all through her like a conduit. They were making her into a bridge, she'd said. It felt as though the construction were almost complete, with her body and soul strung all through it. Anguish rose up inside me, overriding the sensations she was sending to me.

How the hell could I pull her away from that without hurting her even more?

"There," she murmured, and an image flitted through my head of a tall, glittering office building. Something heavy and ominous rested in a pair of hands. Exhilaration rippled in the air as figures marched toward the place together.

"And there." A public square I recognized from the business district, with tramway tracks running along one side. A few café owners were just setting out their signs and wiping off their patio chairs. A malicious glee reached me with the thudding of a pulse in anticipation.

The cult was making another move. Getting into place to wreak more havoc—right now, right here in the city.

"We have to stop them," I said, urgency flaring in my chest.

"I can't," my sister said, her tone so hopeless it tore at my heart. "I'm buried under, broken. I can't do anything. They want to rip me even farther open—but maybe you —if you can get to them—"

Yes. I had to get out of here, out of this daze, and bring hell down on the cult before they did the same to us.

My dream arms flailed out in the sleep-like haze. I

clawed toward consciousness. Up, out, eyes open, mind clear—if I just reached far enough, strained hard enough…

I flung myself right back into awareness with a gasp for breath. My body knifed upward on the bed. Bash grasped my shoulder to steady me, and the words tumbled hoarse from my throat.

"The cult is planning more attacks—getting in place right now. I'm not sure about one of the spots, but the other's near here." I spun to find Garrett straightening up in the room's chair. "You have to tell the police to get over there, catch them before they do anything."

He jumped to his feet. "I'll get my phone. Do you know what the people look like? What exactly they're going to do?"

I shook my head with a clench of my gut. "All I know is the places." I described the building I'd caught a glimpse of and told him the name of the square, and he hustled out of Bash's room.

My pulse hadn't stopped thudding. I slid off the bed, still a bit dizzy from the pill but with adrenaline cutting through its effects.

"We should go too. To the square. I'd probably recognize the cultists before the police do. I don't know how much time we have."

"Of course." Bash grabbed a car key off the bedside table. He'd dressed while I drifted in my artificial sleep, maybe anticipating that I might need more from him soon.

When we came out, Garrett was heading back down the hall toward us, speaking in a low but intense voice into his phone. He'd thrown on a pair of slacks and a shirt he hadn't yet buttoned. At the sight of us, he picked up his pace to catch up, with a nod as if he'd guessed what we were doing.

"I understand that the chief isn't there yet," he said into the phone. "You still have officers in the field and on call, don't you? Get them out there. We're lucky we got any advance information at all."

I glanced at the door to Sherlock and John's suite, but it'd be a tight fit with all of us in the one car, and Bash and I alone should have been able to take on a handful of cultists if need be. Let them get a little more sleep.

As we hustled down the stairs, skipping the wait for the elevator, Garrett hung up with a grimace. "They're sending people over. I don't know if they believed the situation was quite as urgent as I tried to tell them. Are we going to try to beat them there?"

"Better than sitting around doing nothing," I said. "I could feel my sister when I was talking to her—feel how the fiends have been working on her, manipulating her body to their ends… I don't think it's going to take much for them to push through with their plans. If we can even stall one of this morning's missions, it could buy us time we'll need."

On the street outside, Bash dropped into the driver's seat of the used car he'd bought cheap for our activities here that didn't involve much cargo. Garrett didn't object to my taking the other front seat. Bash gunned the engine as the detective scrambled into the back.

I consulted my mental map of the city. "Take the second left. That street should get us there the fastest."

Bash pulled onto the road, quiet in the expanding dawn, and took off with a roar that sounded thunderous. I scanned the sidewalks as we sped along, watching for any figures who pinged on my cult radar. Should we swing by their tower in case there were more sneaking out on similar errands? But the figures Olivia had conveyed to me had already been getting into place. We couldn't risk wasting any time.

Lord only knew what the bastards meant to do. My stomach turned at the memory of the vicious impression I'd gotten from the emotions that had briefly grazed mine.

Bash tore around the corner and swerved around a few slower cars rumbling along ahead of us. I leaned forward in my seat. It shouldn't take more than five minutes to reach the square at this time of day, especially at the speed he was going. Then we just needed to spot the perps, and—

Garrett's phone rang. He yanked it to his ear. "Yes?"

There was a long silence with nothing but the rumble of the engine. My heart started to sink. Then Garrett let out a curse so choked that my hopes slipped away completely.

"It's too late," he said to us. "It's already happened. They weren't going after the buildings this time, not really. Three different sites around the city, including that square —they just opened fire on everyone in the area, on the windows of the shops and the apartments overhead… The police are only just arriving on the scenes, but at least a dozen people are dead."

# CHAPTER NINETEEN

*Garrett*

The local police commander's accent grew thicker when he was frustrated.

"I can't order a raid on an entire business complex just because a foreign officer said so, Mr. Lestrade," he said over the phone. "The culprits weren't traced from the building, and we've found no identification that would allow us to connect them to it. I want to see an end to this violence as much as you do, but my hands are tied."

I was starting to see why Sherlock often got irritated with my insistence on staying within legal bounds. I sank back into the sofa in his and John's suite, grimacing at the wall. "Between the three attacks, you've now got nearly forty deaths that happened in the space of a few minutes. They've already escalated their attacks once. Do you really want to find out what they'll do next if we don't step in?"

"We're doing everything we can. If you can provide a clear link to the building, we'll act immediately. I have superiors to answer to."

Didn't we all? Maybe it *was* easier for me to argue with him when mine were thousands of miles distant. That didn't ease the anxiety tangled in my gut. But this conversation wasn't getting us anywhere.

"I'll see what I can do," I said, and hung up with a sigh.

"No luck?" Jemma said from where she'd been pacing the living area. For a brief while last night, she'd looked content. She'd looked *happy*. Now her face was as clouded as her pensive gray eyes.

She hadn't said it, and I doubted she'd admit it out loud, but I'd been in enough fraught situations like this to recognize the signs. She blamed herself for not figuring out sooner what the cultists meant to do, for not getting there fast enough to stop them.

"They can't prove the perps from the shootings had anything to do with the tower," I said. "So they can't justify any kind of building-wide action. If their people had been watching the place more closely..."

"As everywhere, we can't count on official channels for the most effective action," Sherlock said in his matter-of-fact way.

Normally a comment like that would have raised my hackles, but at the moment I couldn't help agreeing.

"What steps can we take at this point?" John asked, coming over to the dining table with a cup of tea he'd just poured. "We've treaded outside the law to take down communes before."

Bash scowled where he was leaning against the sofa near Jemma, his gaze following her movements through the room. "It's a lot easier setting a community up for a fall when they're out in the wilderness without walls or security systems and all that protecting them. All we needed before was stealth and good timing, and we didn't have to worry about any neighbors spotting us and getting nervous. This is much more complicated."

"And the tower commune must have noticed the increased police presence by now." Jemma stopped in the middle of the room with a frustrated exhalation. "They *couldn't* have all snuck out without alerting anyone unless they realized the building was under surveillance and purposefully took steps to evade the cops. Which means they'll be on high alert inside, too. If I'd taken a stab at it a couple days ago…"

My chest tightened. She wasn't just blaming herself for this morning—she was convincing herself she should have gone on what would essentially have been a suicide mission, alone and without half the support we'd arranged.

"You might not have gotten more than two steps beyond the lift," Sherlock said baldly. "They may have increased their defenses, but we've come up with several techniques for breaking those down. I expect the balance will lean in our favor." He glanced at his phone and then at John. "Speaking of which, aren't we due to gather that order from the warehouse shortly?"

The doctor mumbled a curse and took a large gulp from his tea before leaving it on the table. "I lost track of the time." He nodded to the rest of us. "It shouldn't take more than an hour. This is the last of the equipment. Then we can lay out the full strategy and be ready to tackle them by tomorrow."

Neither Jemma nor Bash looked all that comforted by his comment. As they ducked out, Jemma started pacing again.

"We don't even know how well most of those

techniques are going to work," she muttered. "I've never tried them before. We could *all* be walking into a total slaughter."

I hesitated for a second and then got up from the sofa. We were in this together now. She'd agreed to hold off on the self-sacrificing approach, trusting that we had a better chance working as a group. She'd come to me last night— she'd wanted that connection. And God, I'd wanted it too. Why the hell should I hold back on showing how I felt now?

I caught her in mid-pace, gently grasping her hands as I looked her in the eyes, knowing better than to assume a full embrace would comfort her.

"Hey," I said. "You've been doing everything you can. There might have been even more attacks today if we hadn't alerted the police as quickly as we were able to. We're going to kick these bastards right out of our world and throw away whatever key has been letting them come back in. They don't stand a chance against the five of us."

Her laugh came out rough. "There's a hell of a lot more than five of them. And they've been preparing for this moment for an awfully long time, from what I can tell. I had no idea—I never thought—"

She pulled away from me with a strangled noise and stalked to the other end of the room. Bash's gaze continued to follow her, but he didn't try to stop her. I guessed he could tell it wouldn't help.

"We've got the tools to completely fuck with their set-up now," he said instead. "You haven't used those strategies before? That's a good thing. It means they can't expect them. We'll shock the hell out of them. That gives us plenty of advantage."

"And how many more people are going to die before

we get the chance to try?" Jemma said, glaring at the mirror over the desk. "There were three kids this morning —one of them was only five. If they launch another attack in the middle of the day instead of that early, there'll probably be even more."

Oh. I hadn't even considered that dimension to her distress. In every kid the shrouded folk or their minions hurt, she saw her sister.

"You're right," I said with a rush of conviction. "There has to be something more we can do to protect people." I was a goddamned cop—out of the bunch of us, I should be able to figure out how to get the local law enforcement on our side.

If only we could have come up with an angle like in Scotland, where we'd gotten the police to raid the place out of concern for their well-being rather than evidence of crimes. But that had required a set-up we couldn't pull off in the middle of a city without being caught.

The whole scenario had been different, though. We hadn't needed to worry about anyone's immediate safety outside of the commune. Here, the cultists had innocent people working right below them, maybe even living among them for all we knew.

An idea sparked in my head with a ripple of exhilaration. I sucked in a breath. "Jemma, it doesn't matter if the cult knows we're onto them, does it? Because you believe they already know that?"

She turned to study me. "I don't think we should show too much of our hand, but no, I don't think it'll be any surprise to them to know we've marked their location and that we're probably planning *something*."

"Then why don't we set the police on the people who *aren't* part of it?"

Bash gave me a puzzled look. "What are you talking about?"

I made a vague gesture in the air. "The Istanbul police can't take the actual criminals into custody because there's no proof they're criminals right now. Fine. So let's remove the commune's most immediate potential targets. If we present the police with a course of action that's about saving people's lives rather than arresting them, they're less likely to balk. All they need to do is make up an excuse to evacuate the building. Tell the tenants there's an issue with the electrical system or the plumbing or whatever makes the most sense. I doubt they'll go around banging on people's doors forcing people to leave, but—"

Jemma's eyes widened, but she was smiling. "Everyone who doesn't have a higher agenda wrapped up in the building won't need to be forced. They'll go because they're told. We'll get all the innocents out of the way before we go after the commune."

Her obvious approval brought a grin to my own lips. "And it'll also make it harder for the commune to arrange any further attacks. Once the tower is officially evacuated, the police monitoring it will have to assume *anyone* who leaves the building is part of the cult."

"What are you waiting for, then? Get them on it."

The commander wasn't exactly happy to hear from me again, but when I laid out the plan and emphasized the potential carnage avoided, he gradually warmed to it. "I'm not sure how long we can keep up the ruse," he warned me. "There are limits to how much we can deceive people even for their own safety."

"I understand," I told him. "We're hoping to have a more permanent solution very soon." One he wouldn't approve of, but he wouldn't need to know the details—or anything at all about it until after we were either through to the other side or dead.

By the time I'd hung up, tomorrow's looming mission had overshadowed most of my triumph at the gambit I'd come up with. Evacuating the building really was just a stop-gap measure. And Jemma was right: We didn't know how well any of our experimental techniques would work against the cult or their masters.

But maybe there was a way to find out.

I grabbed my laptop from where I'd left it on the side table and brought up my files from the task force. Police forces from all over the world had sent in data that matched the patterns I'd laid out to get outside confirmation that they had cultists in the area—and what exact area the commune was likely to be in. I'd gotten some from officers in this region before I'd even shown up here. Not for anything within the city, but…

There. My grin came back. I looked up and found Jemma watching me, warily but with obvious interest.

"You want to make sure we can crash the party in the tower tomorrow?" I said. "We can give all this equipment we've been gathering a trial run tonight. I'm pretty sure there's a commune just a few hours outside Istanbul."

Hope lit in Jemma's eyes. "All right. Let's get warmed up."

# CHAPTER TWENTY

*Jemma*

Because there was only one shrouded folk-deflecting cuff and I was the one most used to wearing it, a lot of the heavy lifting for tonight's endeavor fell on me. Carting the sound system and the projectors around the spot where we'd identified a tiny mountainside commune would have been easier with a vehicle, but that would have caught someone's attention. So I carried the equipment a couple pieces at a time on foot through the dry forestland that covered the slope.

A crisp sap smell tickled my nose in the cooling night air. I scanned the forest around me and set the amplifier and its power source into a nook between two tree roots, the volume turned up as high as it would go. Hopefully that would be loud enough to blare all the way to the commune. I hadn't let myself go close enough to need to deal with whatever guards they had staked out around the place.

That was the last speaker in the ring around the commune. I straightened up with a roll of my shoulders, both to stretch the muscles and to try to release the tension that had gathered in them.

If this didn't work, if the strategies we'd come up with barely affected the shrouded folk and their worshippers, then we were back to square one when it came to tackling the creeps in the tower. It was better to find that out now rather than in a much tighter situation, but the thought still made my stomach knot.

I loped back to the truck we'd parked at the edge of the forested area. My men were waiting for me there, John and Garrett already stirring restlessly as they waited for my return, Bash keeping his usual cool composure. Sherlock was standing out beside the truck too, but he didn't have anything to be anticipating. While the four of us tackled the commune, he was hanging back here. Partly to activate the speakers on cue, but also partly because John had insisted.

"Even with your fighting experience, that arm is going to hold you back too much," he'd said on the drive over. "From the activity around the place, there can't be many people living there. The four of us should be able to handle them just fine." And when Sherlock had started to protest, he'd added, "I didn't kick up a fuss when you insisted that *I* stay back while you and Bash put yourselves into comas to go after Jemma."

Sherlock had grumbled a little, but he'd accepted his friend's judgment after that point.

Now, I gave them an all-clear gesture as I approached. We'd already discussed how we'd position ourselves for the raid, each of us carrying stun guns and tasers, but before they headed off my nerves compelled me to make a final reminder.

"We don't want to let *anyone* make it out of the commune. The guards go down first, then the sound and lights display kicks off once we're in the settlement and can keep track of the other inhabitants. If any of them slips away and warns the commune in the tower about what we're doing, we could be screwed even if this works."

The guys nodded and set off to form a loose circle around our target. I stayed at the truck with Sherlock, which was a welcome rest after all the trekking around of various equipment.

I hopped up on the hood with my radio ready for the guys to let me know they were in position. Sherlock leaned his good arm onto the truck next to me, studying the forest as if it might tell him ahead of time how this encounter would play out.

"I'm sorry," I said. "Technically it's my fault you have to sit out."

He glanced at his cast and gave a rueful shake of his head. "It's because of you I'm a part of this mission at all, so I'd have to say on the balance I still owe you."

"For getting you sucked into a case that's a hundred times more dangerous than anything you've faced in the past?"

Sherlock made an incredulous sound. "I don't evaluate the value of a case based on how little peril I personally risk. My life's work is finding the ones where my expertise and intellect is necessary to unraveling the mystery and where the greatest number of people stand to benefit from that unraveling. This scenario is both incredibly obtuse and exceptionally catastrophic. I'll consider it the pinnacle of my career if I contribute in any meaningful way to preventing that catastrophe."

"Let's certainly hope there aren't greater heights for you to reach in the future, then," I teased.

"I think perhaps I might enjoy a few more pedestrian cases in the aftermath, if only to cleanse my palate," the detective allowed.

I looked at him in the twilight, watching his expression carefully. The question had been niggling at me for a while, but this line of conversation brought it to the forefront. "When you joined in with the others to convince me we should tackle this situation together… Am I really going to hold all that much interest to you once we're finished with the shrouded folk? Or was *your* goal mainly about getting to play a part right now?"

Sherlock blinked at me with a bemusement that reassured me more than I'd realized I needed. "Why would you think that?"

"*I'm* not much of a mystery anymore, am I? You've unraveled me. What's left to be fascinated by?"

He let out a bark of a laugh. "I find it hard to believe you'll fail to find new ways of engaging my attention. Besides, John is hardly a mystery, and I haven't stopped appreciating his company." His eyebrows rose slightly. "Are you asking because you're finding yourself becoming bored with *me*?"

Every part of me protested at how ridiculous that idea was. In who else would I find a mind this precise and agile, that could keep me on my toes and meet every feint and parry I made with one of his own?

Which, of course, was obviously the same point he'd been making in relation to me.

I scooted back to lean against the windshield, mostly

satisfied. But his question still deserved a thoughtful answer.

"No," I said. "But to the others, it's more of a romance. They've all expressed, in their own ways, a certain… depth of feeling that fits with a long-term commitment. You and I aren't people inclined to make our decisions based on emotion, are we?" I thought of Olivia. "Other than in rare circumstances. At least, I assume I won't be getting any declarations of love from you."

Would I want to? I wasn't entirely sure. It was so difficult to picture it happening that I had trouble judging how I'd feel about it, both bizarre and a little thrilling at the same time.

"Perhaps not," Sherlock said with a nod. "But what is 'love' other than a word that means different things to every speaker? It's hardly an objective stimulus that one can identify with certainty. I'd propose that it means much more that I can say I look forward to every conversation we have, that I find myself constantly stimulated—in one way or another—in your presence, and that I've come to understand you well enough that I can easily accept even an apparently horrifying transgression."

It was such a perfect response, and perfectly Sherlockian, that an unexpected flutter passed through my chest. Right then, if only for a few seconds, maybe there was enough room in me that I could have said I loved him. Those seconds were fleeting, though. Instead, I said, "I believe it does. And in case there was any doubt, all those sentiments are returned."

"I don't recall ever making any horrifying

transgressions on you," he said dryly, but the glint that came into his eyes was pleased.

"You interrupted my quest to rescue my sister very clearly against my desires," I pointed out. "And without really having any idea how much trouble you could be causing for me."

"A gamble I made with much the same confidence in my abilities to mitigate that damage as you had when you pushed me down that cliff." Sherlock smiled at me. "So yes, I suppose there is an equivalency there."

My earpiece crackled, and Garrett's voice traveled through. "I'm in position now."

I straightened up on the hood, checking my weapons. It was only a few more minutes before John spoke up too. "I've arrived."

Bash had the farthest to go, taking the spot at the complete opposite end of this area, but he was also the fastest of the guys. I'd only just finished making a final examination of the broadcasting equipment in the truck when he called in too. "Ready to go."

I tugged my light jacket down to my hips. "All right. Let's move. Call in again when you're sure you've disabled any guards in your range."

"I'll be waiting for your signal," Sherlock said. He hopped into the back of the truck.

I kept my breaths slow and even as I set off into the woods again. Based on the data Garrett's associates had uncovered, I doubted this commune held more than twenty people total. They wouldn't have more than a few on guard. They might even be more complacent right now, thinking our attention was focused on the urban incidents.

About five minutes past the ring of speakers I'd set

out, I spotted my first guard. I slowed, setting my feet carefully, and flexed my fingers at my sides.

I expected John and Garrett would stick to stunning any they came across. I had no qualms about snapping their necks. The shrouded folk might have commanded their followers, but the people had minds of their own, and with those minds they'd decided to torment each other and any kids born into the place. People from this spot might even have traveled to Istanbul to help with the shootings there.

The guy ahead of me held a revolver at his side. I slipped around him and slunk up behind him, my body tensed for the maneuver. He started to shift his weight—and I grasped his head with a sharp twist of my arms.

His spine cracked. I guided his limp body down to the ground so it wouldn't make too loud a thump.

"One down at the south end," I murmured into my mic.

"I just took down one here in the north," Bash said.

There was silence from the other two for a short time as I crept closer to the actual commune. Then Garrett said, in a tight voice that didn't hide his discomfort, "One down here in the east. I haven't seen anyone else around."

"I haven't come across any guards at all," John said. "I can see a building now through the trees. Maybe there were only the three."

"Let's be sure." I started to veer to the side. "Bash, head west, and we can check the edges of his section."

I didn't come across any other guards in my prowl, and neither did my hitman. "Pretty small outfit," he remarked.

"As we expected," I said. "All right. Up to the edge."

We eased through the forest toward the area where

scattered trees had been cut down to make room for the commune's buildings. It wasn't exactly a clearing, because they'd left some vegetation for cover, but once out there, we'd be able to see anyone who tried to flee. I stopped a few paces from the nearest building, the silence thick around me, and whispered, "Here."

One after the other, the men reported in. I braced myself, popping out my earpiece to replace it with plugs as the others should be doing and slipping my fingers around my taser. Then I said, "Sherlock, let them have it."

The soundtrack we'd put together blared from the planted speakers so loud that I flinched even though I'd expected it. Drums pounded out a beat composed of multiple patterns; voices pontificated in iambic pentameter; a rhythmic stomping overshadowed it all. The noise blended together into a weird sort of harmony that any shrouded one should be repulsed by—and any human being without any ear protection should be disoriented by. Overhead, projected lights formed a gigantic Fibonacci sequence against the sky.

As cultists started bursting from their huts, I lunged into the commune. I zapped a woman with a rifle first. As she fell, I grabbed the gun and spun to slam the butt into the head of a man who'd charged at me.

Shouts penetrated the onslaught of sound faintly. I stunned another man who stumbled out of his hut bleary-eyed and dashed deeper into the settlement.

The noise was definitely affecting the cultists. A woman in front of me swayed as she swiveled on her feet, her face scrunched with discomfort. She barely seemed to see me before I knocked her down. If any fiends had been lurking around their worshippers, they'd been driven away —I didn't catch so much of a whiff of their putrid scent.

I sprinted around another hut and found Bash and Garrett shocking two cultists who'd emerged from neighboring buildings. Then whatever teamwork that effort had involved fell apart.

Bash motioned for Garrett to drag the cultists into one of the huts. Garrett frowned and shook his head with a wave toward the other buildings.

He was right—the plan had been that we'd make sure we'd caught all the cultists before we worried about confining them. But Bash stepped toward the detective inspector with a menacing look that made my jaw grit. I hurried over to snap him out of whatever macho mindset he'd gotten into, and the crack of a gunshot split through the blaring rhythms.

The bullet slammed into Bash's shoulder, making his whole torso jerk. My lips parted with a cry, but his military-trained instincts took over in a snap. He threw himself back against the closest building, his head leaping to his real gun in the same motion. His sniper-trained eyes narrowed. Ignoring the blood streaking over his shirt, he fired at someone I couldn't see from where I stood. I knew he'd landed the shot from his grim but satisfied expression as he lowered the gun.

Garrett hesitated and then hurried off to check the rest of the commune. I caught Bash's eye, and he indicated I should keep on with the plan with a brisk gesture before pressing his hand to his shoulder. My gut clenched, but I jogged on to check for stragglers.

It wasn't a life-threatening wound. He'd be all right. But all the relief I'd felt in seeing our gambits succeed had drained away.

He'd gotten distracted with his posturing, his momentary refusal to let one of the other men stick to our plan. The bullet *could* have blasted through a lung or his heart.

How the hell could I be sure we'd make it through an invasion of the tower tomorrow if the five of us still couldn't totally trust each other?

# CHAPTER TWENTY-ONE

*Bash*

My goddamn shoulder still ached. I sank a little deeper into the chair at my hotel room desk and grimaced.

Even when I wasn't moving, a dull pain throbbed right below my shoulder cap where the bullet had passed through. I'd taken a Tylenol 3 I'd had on hand, but I didn't want to risk getting too dopey before our mission-to-end-all-missions tomorrow.

No, I'd already fucked things up enough without that. As much as I disliked the pain, the worst part of the injury was the reminder of how close the shot had come to striking something I couldn't just bandage up and grit my teeth through. And it'd been my own carelessness that'd done it. Caught up in the moment, wanting to take charge and make sure the job was done right *my* way… and failing to notice the enemy just fifteen feet behind me.

Jemma hadn't said anything about it to me while we'd

shut the cultists up in one of their huts or during the drive back. She'd made sure the wound was cleaned and well-bandaged and then leaned against the window to doze through the deepening night. But even when she'd been half asleep, the worry lines had remained on her forehead and at the corners of her mouth.

So much depended on what we did tomorrow. Whether we could pull it off. Whether we could work *together*, as a unit, not some hotshot maverick who thought he was better than teamwork.

I hadn't worked with a full team since my army days, ages ago, and I hadn't really liked it even then. No, being out on my own with my sniper rifle in hand and target in mind had been vastly preferable. But I should damn well be able to cooperate when I had to. I wasn't that nineteen-year-old jackass anymore.

I was better than that. Jemma had believed it. But maybe it was more important that I convinced myself to believe it too.

After tomorrow, I might not be around to be anything at all. Going up against that piddly commune had been nothing compared to launching an assault on the monsters' tower. Before that could happen… there were a couple other people in my life I might owe something to.

I opened up my compact laptop, barely more than a tablet with a keyboard. That was how I liked my computers: small and straightforward. The street beyond my window was pitch-black, the time well past midnight, but that was perfect for a call back to the US. They'd just be getting home from work.

I checked my shirt to make sure the bandage on my shoulder was covered, and then I typed the number I'd gotten via one of our hacker cohorts into my phone. Texting my little sister.

*Hey, Charlotte. It's Bash. I'm sorry for the long silence. Can we talk—maybe a videochat over the computer? I'd like to be able to see your face.*

I hadn't seen her in motion since I'd left her and Sam at our grandparents' house all those years ago. Still photographs didn't quite cut it. She might still say no, though. She might think it was some kind of prank.

Tapping my fingers against the side of the phone, I waited. And waited. Impatience started to prickle up my spine. Then, finally, an answering message popped up.

*Bash? Are you kidding me? Of course. I just walked in the door—give me a second to get everything set up.*

I thought I could read enthusiasm in that response, but it was hard to tell with plain text. My heart thumped heavily as I typed in my account info so she could try to connect. And then I waited again.

It only took a couple minutes this time. The app sounded an alert for the incoming call. A flash of panic washed over me—did I look presentable? What if I said the wrong thing? —but I forced myself to hit the button to accept the call.

And there was my sister staring back at me, her face narrower without its former childhood softness, her eyes not quite as wide but still framed by long lashes, her expression slack with shock. She must be making a similar assessment of me.

I hadn't seen her since she was seven. She hadn't seen me since I was thirteen. I'd grown up a lot since then too.

Not so much that she had any doubts, clearly. "It's really you," she said in a halting voice. She leaned closer to the screen as if she could reach right through it to this room. "Oh my God. Where have you been? Sam and I were worried you were *dead*, that Dad—or some other way— It's been *seventeen* years."

My throat constricted. "I know," I made myself say. My fingers itched to cut off the connection, to slam down the laptop as if that would sever the guilt and the fear too, but I clenched my hand and held it in place. "I'm sorry. At first I just thought it'd be easier for you, staying with Gram and Gramps, if you weren't thinking or worrying about me, and then I got caught up in a bunch of stuff, and… I let it go too long. I didn't want to let it go any longer."

"Well, I'm really, really glad that you're okay." A shimmer came into her eyes that looked like a hint of withheld tears. "And really glad that you tracked me down. How pissed off was Dad after he found out you'd taken us away?"

I didn't often think back to those last few years with my parents before I'd conned my way into the army underage. The truth was Dad had raged about it for a few days and then fallen into his usual routines as if it'd always been just Mom and me around to act as punching bags, verbally or physically. I didn't think it'd help Charlotte any hearing the details. That wasn't what I wanted this conversation to be about anyway.

"He was… Dad," I said. "But I survived, and I got out of there myself pretty soon after, and Mom got away too eventually. Has she been in touch at all?"

"A couple times. I think she was embarrassed that it went on so long, that you were the one who got us out instead of her." She swiped her hand over her mouth and then peered at me more avidly. "Tell me what you've been doing all this time—whatever you can tell me. I want to hear everything."

I wasn't going to tell her *everything*, of course, or even half the things I'd gotten into, but I managed to put an acceptable spin on most of my activities over the last decade and a half. When Charlotte looked satisfied, I prodded her to tell me the things I already knew about her life in her words, plus a few things internet searches hadn't been able to reveal.

The conversation had an awkwardness to it, pauses where one or the other of us grappled with what we'd say, hesitations when we weren't sure how to take a comment, but I couldn't have expected it to go perfectly smoothly. Talking to her still felt *good*, in a way I hadn't even imagined.

I'd done okay by her. Look at this woman she'd grown up to be.

"Are you going to talk to Sam?" she asked before we ended the call.

I nodded. "I figured I owe him too. Maybe... Maybe if I'm back in your area sometime, we could grab a coffee or something."

She smiled. "Yeah. I'd like that."

The call with Sam went a little more awkwardly with a little more frustration on his part over the long silence, but he didn't vent much anger, just pent-up worries. After we signed off, I climbed onto my bed and lay down on top of the covers, letting my mind process everything I'd just experienced.

My siblings didn't hate me. They didn't look at me and automatically see a criminal. I was still their big brother, somehow or other.

The thought both reassured me and gnawed at me. I'd

stepped back into their lives, and I might vanish all over again tomorrow.

Well, I simply couldn't let that happen then, now could I?

The pain in my shoulder had faded a little more, but I couldn't have said I was anywhere near drifting off when a knock sounded on my door. I sat up in an instant.

"Yeah?"

Jemma's voice traveled through. "It's me."

I got up and let her in, that more recent, sharper guilt jabbing through me all over again. She looked tired, her red waves swept back into a braid which left her eyes looking even larger in her pale face, but she walked over to perch on my bed with a typically determined air.

"We can't let what happened tonight happen again tomorrow," she said without preamble.

Had that worry been keeping her up? I swallowed hard. "I agree. I got distracted in the moment—I should have kept better control over myself."

She looked up at me with the same frank, assured gaze she'd had since the moment I first met her years ago, when she was still a teenager. "I need you in there with me. You're the one with the most combat experience. That isn't negotiable. So whoever we need to ask to stay out of the mission so you're not thinking about their performance instead of yours, you have to tell me. We'll figure it out."

I could just imagine how Garrett—or John—or even Sherlock would feel about that. The guilt dug in even deeper. "I know to watch for it now," I said. "I won't react the same way. We're going to need all hands on deck, won't we?"

"Better fewer hands who are all fully focused."

This was my fault. That understanding sank in and

settled like a stone on my gut. *I'd* created a fissure where we'd been building a force to be reckoned with.

That wasn't what I wanted to be for her. I wanted to be the solid foundation she could stand on, the one who held her... and everyone she needed with her... together.

The impulse hit me, sudden and potent enough that I didn't second-guess it. I motioned to the bed. "Relax a few minutes and wait for me. I'll be back. All right?"

Jemma gave me a curious look, but she scooted farther onto the bed so she could sink back against the pillows. "What are you up to all of a sudden, Bash?"

"You'll just have to wait and see, Majesty," I said with all the good humor I could summon through my dampened mood. Then I stepped out into the hall.

My little brother and sister weren't the only family I had left, or the only family I needed to connect with. Jemma was my family more than anyone else in the world now. And it was time I admitted that whatever strange family the two of us had formed had grown in the past few months. It was time I showed her that I could handle that, in every possible way.

I rapped on Garrett's door first. He opened it looking rather tired himself but still in his clothes, so obviously he hadn't been having the easiest time getting to bed. Despite the way I'd hassled him in the commune, when I said, "Come on. There's something we need to do," he trusted me enough to follow. Which maybe was all I had to know.

When John opened the suite's door, I could see Sherlock standing by the table, where two glasses of what I'd bet was sherry sat. They'd stayed up hashing over tomorrow's plans, no doubt.

"What's this about?" Sherlock asked when I repeated the request.

"Jemma," I said, and that was enough to shift him the two doors down the hall to my room.

Jemma sat up from her lounging pose when we came in, her gaze sliding over all of us with an expression both puzzled and intrigued. "You thought we should have a group meeting?" she said. "There's more room for that in the suite."

"No," I said. "I think we all need to be one hundred percent clear on how committed we are to collaborating. On how committed we are to *you*. I'm not out to have you all to myself, Mori." My mouth went slightly dry. "Not when I knew everyone in this room brings something into your life. Makes you happy. If you're up for it, I want to see how just how satisfied you can be when you've got all of us at your disposal." I glanced around at the other men. "Unless any of you has an objection."

Garrett swallowed audibly, but a spark of excitement had already lit in his eyes. "None here."

A flush crept over John's cheeks. "Well, I... I guess it would be good to find out how well we can, er, work together."

As usual, I found Sherlock difficult to read, but it was clear from his answer that he wasn't against the idea anyway. "An interesting proposition," he said. "It has seemed that two can provoke more pleasure than one, so *four...*"

Jemma wet her lips. She shot me a quick but brilliant smile that melted most of the guilt still lodged inside me. "I think I'm ready to find out."

She stayed where she was, waiting for us to come to her—understandably, since she was already on the bed. I didn't want to step in right away in case it looked as if I were staking some kind of claim despite everything I'd said.

To my surprise, John moved first. He leaned his walking stick against the bedside table and climbed onto the bed next to Jemma. She tipped her head, and he took the invitation to kiss her.

That kiss jolted everyone else to action. Garrett came around the other side of the bed to sit at Jemma's other side, slipping a hand around her waist and kissing her shoulder. Sherlock settled himself near the end of the bed and eased one of Jemma's socks off before beginning to massage her foot.

I hung back for a moment, deciding where I best fit in. Jemma was beaming with an exhilarated flush as she turned her head from John to Garrett, and part of me would have liked to stay there and simply watch her immerse herself in the other men's attentions. But I was part of this bizarre family too, and that meant taking my place alongside them.

Jemma had pushed herself away from the pillows. I tossed a couple of them aside to make more room and dropped down behind her, running my hand up her back. She leaned into my touch as she kissed Garrett and stroked her fingers down John's chest, and even though I'd thought going through with this might be hard, instead I felt nothing but how right this was. For her to be admired and cherished—and, yeah, *loved*—in every possible way.

She'd spent so long having to shut everyone around her out to protect herself, and now she was letting four of us in. And I had the honor of being one of those four. That was pretty fucking amazing.

I teased my hands down her sides and grasped the

hem of her sleeveless blouse to lift it off her. The other men shifted as I tugged it over her head. Then I was sliding my hands around to the bare skin of her belly, and John was claiming her mouth again, and Garrett was snapping her bra loose before lowering his mouth to her breast. Jemma hummed encouragingly, so low it was almost a purr.

Sherlock had just finished tending to her other foot. He fondled her legs from calves to knees, slowly working his way upward. When he reached her upper thigh, she made an impatient sound with a buck of her hips. He chuckled and reached to undo her pants.

Jemma sat up on her knees to shed her slacks and her panties. She glanced around at us with an imperious look. "If I'm calling the shots here, I'd like to see a lot less clothes on all of you."

We all took a moment to shed shirts and pants. I scooted to the side so I could claim Jemma's mouth for myself, and she kissed me back hard, her fingers gliding up over my scalp in the most delicious caress.

Garrett cupped her between her legs until she was swaying and moaning at his touch. Then he bent down on the bed to bring his mouth to her clit. As I lowered my head to provoke her breasts with the heat of my mouth and swipes of my tongue, Sherlock leaned in for a kiss, and John ran his hands over her ass.

"Condom?" he said in a ragged voice.

"In the drawer," Jemma said with a vague motion and a gasp as Garrett tilted his head. "Be quick about it."

John chuckled and did as he was told. Her breath hitched as he slid into her from behind. Between him inside her, Garrett's oral attentions, and Sherlock and I trailing our hands over every other inch of her, she was already trembling in that way I knew meant she was close to coming. And God, what a spectacular coming I expected it'd be.

Jemma gripped my arm, her hips rocking between her one lover's thrusts and the other's lips. Sherlock nipped her shoulder and rolled her nipple with his thumb, and she yanked his mouth back to hers. Then she was urging him upright with one hand while the other traced a tantalizing path down my chest to the bulge tenting my boxers.

I could feel her muscles quivering with the building bliss, but she held on to bring us with her. As she freed Sherlock's rigid cock and sucked it into her mouth, she dipped her hand inside my boxers to grasp my erection. I mumbled a curse and kissed a path along her shoulder.

For all the sensations that must have been rushing through her, her grip stayed steady. She pumped me firmly but tenderly, swiveling the heel of her hand over the tip in a way that made me groan.

It didn't take long before my balls tightened. I stroked her breasts and her back, willing every ounce of pleasure I could into her body to offer back what she was doing to me. Her fingers pressed against the underside of my cock, and I came with a choked sound and a giddy rush that shot right through the top of my head.

Somewhere during my hazy afterglow, Sherlock's breath caught with the shudder of his own release. Jemma's head tipped back toward John, he sped up his pace, and her body shook with the force of her orgasm racing through her. I got half hard again just seeing it. John bowed his head next to hers from behind as he must have reached his own peak.

As Jemma's body started to slump with satisfaction

between us, she looked to Garrett, who'd raised his head with a pleased grin. "I'm good, Firecracker," he told her. "This was about you, not us."

That was true, but it had been about the four of us at the same time. About sprawling around her without feeling in any particular hurry to go anywhere else. About not getting uptight if my arm brushed Sherlock's shoulder or Garrett's knee bumped my ankle. About seeing how spectacular this interlude had been, *because* we were all here.

The other three men hadn't just contributed to Jemma's happiness. If I was being honest, they'd each given a new dimension to my life too. When I set anything like jealousy aside, I had to admit I appreciated Sherlock's smarts, John's generosity, and Garrett's stubbornness.

If we were her family, then we were each other's too.

"We'll all be there tomorrow," I said to Jemma, stroking her hair. "You can count on all of us."

This time, she didn't argue with me, only snuggled deeper into the nest between us as if we'd always been so united.

*Jemma*

One benefit of having the tower's offices evacuated was we didn't have much competition for the use of the elevators. I popped the maintenance hatch in the ceiling of one car and scrambled up onto its roof without needing to worry about onlookers.

Bash and Garrett clambered after me. John gave us a playful salute that contrasted with his tense expression before he helped click the hatch back in place. We'd decided that since we'd probably need people on the ground running interference with the regular citizens and possibly the police once our lights and sounds display kicked into gear, it made sense for the two members of our group who'd have the most trouble climbing a couple dozen stories to take that role.

We still might not have much time once the show started. The three of us were all carrying custom decals and portable speakers in our backpacks, but most of our equipment we'd had to put in place using the surrounding buildings and other city structures. The general population probably wouldn't be too happy once we started blasting our bizarre soundtrack.

I adjusted the pack's straps on my shoulders over the padding of my bulletproof vest, exchanged a nod with the other two to confirm we were ready, and gripped the cool metal rungs to start my upward climb. This part, the pure physical exertion with the uncertainty of what exactly we'd find on the other side of the elevator doors above, was my least favorite part of the plan. The sooner we could get to kicking cultist ass, the happier I'd be.

My muscles remembered the tempo I'd found when I'd climbed higher in the shaft before. This trip from the ground floor might be twice as far, but I could handle that. I kept a steady pace, centering my weight on my legs as much as I could, taking deep breaths of the cool still air.

The maintenance lights formed an eerie glow around us. The only sound right now was the murmur of our breaths and the rasp of our shoes against the rungs.

We were starting our assault at the very top, because I was almost certain that was where the shrouded folk were holding Olivia, but that didn't mean we could forget about the floors below. The second this urban commune realized they were under attack, we'd face a counter-attack from every person on hand. I was going to plow through anyone who got in my way until I found my sister and the bridge the fiends were building through her. Bash and Garrett would cover me.

Garrett had balked a little at the rifle Bash had handed him when we'd been suiting up, but he had a stun gun too. "Don't pretend you can get away with just knocking them out if the fighting gets too fraught," I'd said to him. "You want me to get through this alive? I want you to survive it too. If you feel any guilt, just remember the kids you've seen at the other communes, the photos and all that. The people here have done as much or worse. They want to give the monsters free access to our world to turn it into their bloody playground."

The reminder had brought the resolve back into his expression. I didn't think he'd hesitate when the bastards came at him.

*I'm coming,* I thought to my sister now, even though I didn't know if she could sense anything inside my head while I was awake. *I'm finally coming back for you the way I promised.*

As we reached the highest floors, a hint of the shrouded folk scent, dry and sour, tickled my nose. My shoulders stiffened. I climbed faster. It could be just a lingering odor from their periodic visits to the commune, or—

The smell thickened at the same moment as a vibration echoed through the wall. My head jerked down in time to see Bash swing to the side, only keeping his hold on the maintenance ladder by one hand. My pulse stuttered, and I slammed my hand on the device dangling from my belt.

It sent a signal directly to Sherlock and John outside. A second later, the cacophony of sound we'd inflicted on the forest commune yesterday boomed through the walls. Thank God for the ear plugs we'd carefully equipped ourselves with ahead of time. My eardrums ached even with that layer of protection.

Bash regained his balance with no sign of another

blow. The rhythmic noises and the patterns that'd now be projected on the outside of the building must have done the trick to repel the shrouded folk. We'd lost any of the surprise element in our attack, though. I hauled myself up the last distance to the elevator's top entrance as quickly as I could, my muscles straining, and smacked a small explosive against the seam in the middle of the doors before ducking out of range.

The explosive went off with a crash to rival the racket from outside. The force wrenched the doors apart with a gush of smoke to momentarily disguise our arrival, although the cultists would figure it out soon enough. I leapt up the rungs and sprang through the opening, the guys right behind me.

Gunfire crackled through the smoke. I dropped to the floor and swung out my leg to topple a figure that staggered toward us. With a sharp kick, I cracked his neck. Spinning around, I wrenched one of the portable speakers from my pack, shoved it against the wall, and hit the power button. The sounds from outside flooded the hazy room even louder than before.

Garrett had just zapped a woman who'd lunged at us with a carving knife, and Bash fired his pistol at someone farther into the room. I clapped a few decals onto the walls and threw myself back onto my feet.

The smoke was clearing. I took down a couple other armed figures with my own pistol as I scanned the room. It was wide open if dimly light from the shuttered windows, the vacant area stretching across the entire top floor—other than a room built in the center of the space.

My fingers tightened around the gun. I ran for that room, trusting the guys to have my back.

I didn't see any sign of the shrouded folk themselves

intervening again, and the noise was obviously affecting the cultists here just like it had at the other commune last night. One guy with a rifle stumbled as he tried to swing it toward me and then collapsed with one of Bash's bullets in his skull. A woman burst from the stairwell across the room and promptly tripped over her own feet and sprawled on her hands and knees. A couple of older teens hunched in one corner, their hands clamped over their ears.

That didn't give me completely smooth passage, though. As I raced toward my goal, a figure charged toward me. I dodged to the side in time for one of my men to get in a shot—and plowed straight into a woman who'd flung herself around the side of the central room.

She was holding a pistol, and she'd have needed to be essentially dead to miss at that range. Her first shot fired right against my side, jolting me enough through the bulletproof vest that I lost the grip I'd tried to get on her arm. I managed to smack at her hand just as she pulled the trigger again, but I wasn't quite fast enough. The bullet tore through the flesh of my inner thigh. Pain seared along the its path.

I bit my tongue against a cry and shoved the woman to the side before she could make another attempt. My gun hand whipped up at the same time. I shot her between the eyes.

I limped on toward the room as fast as my legs would carry me, searching for the entrance. My thigh kept burning and the fabric below the wound dampened with a steady flow of blood. She might have nicked an artery. I didn't have time to stop to bandage it. That could wait until I got Olivia the hell out of here.

More shots rang out behind me, mingling with shouts

and the blare of our recordings. I tuned it all out when my gaze caught on the outline of a door in the room's far wall.

A heavy padlock held it shut. I had to fire two shots at it to break through. My jaw clenching against the agony spreading through my leg and pelvis, I pushed it open and shuffled inside.

The door swung shut automatically, and the sounds from outside fell away. The sickening stench of the shrouded folk flooded my lungs, so thick I had to stop myself from gagging. A ruddy glow filled my vision. As I leaned on my good leg, I popped out one of my earplugs. Even then, all I could make out was a warble, but I should be able to hear if anyone tried to come after me.

I blinked in the crimson light, trying to clear my eyes. My gaze stalled on the form in the center of that room, the air in my lungs congealing with horror.

The glow was coming from that… thing. A thing that was a column made of lumps of skin and tattered cloth, melted like tree roots into the floor and stretching up to touch the room's low ceiling. The red light rippled through it in an erratic pulse that set my nerves on edge even as my stomach turned. Glowing streaks arced across the ceiling—five of them, like the ring of five keystones in the shrouded realm.

The form shifted, and I made out two pale eyes in the middle of the mass.

I couldn't hold it back then—my gut heaved, and I vomited the small lunch I'd forced down. The liquid mess splattered the floor with a sharper throbbing through my thigh and the sting of stomach acid in my throat.

"Jemma?" the thing said in a quavering rasp.

It was my sister. Or at least, my sister was part of it. When I forced myself to look at it again, I made out the outline of her face, the knob of a chin, the streaks of flaxen hair merging with the column of flesh. Were those her arms, lifted over her head and stretched toward the ceiling, melded together and expanded to encompass that glow from within? Was that a knee partway down the tattered trunk?

The glow flowed through her with its dissonant flickering, even flashing behind those pleading eyes.

"Olivia," I said, barely managing more than a croak. "What did they do to you?"

"I'm the bridge," she said. Her voice wavered with the glow. "I'm here and not. I'm human and them. I bind the worlds together. It's—" A breath rattled out of her. "It's almost complete."

The door behind me started to open. My heart lurched, and I flung myself back against it. It slammed shut, blood pattering onto the floor from where it had saturated my pants. Each thump of my pulse came with a stabbing like shards of glass.

Someone pounded on the door from the other side. I braced my feet against the floor as solidly as I could and clutched my pistol in case I had to shoot whoever was trying to enter.

"How do I get you out?" I said, ignoring the wave of nausea when I looked at my sister again. "I don't want to hurt you." She was so tangled up in whatever the hell the shrouded folk had turned her into, so fused with the room, I couldn't even see where the monstrosity ended and she began. I pictured trying to carve her out and blood gushing forth in a torrent.

"Jemma." Olivia sounded a little choked now. "You can't. I'm here. I'm this. You have to end it. You have to end *me*. That's the only way I can escape."

The horror before was nothing compared to the revulsion that swelled inside me now. "No. I came here to *save* you. I promised I'd come back for you, get you away from them. There has to be a way."

The door shuddered behind me. My feet slid an inch in the pool of blood creeping across the floor.

"This is how you save me," Olivia said. "You have to let me go. Please. I don't want to be what they've made me into. I want to be done."

She'd said something like that before, but I hadn't realized just how final the statement had been. Every bone in my body balked. "I can't. We'll figure it out. We'll kill all the bastards out there and then we can talk it through—"

"There's nothing to figure out. I know. Please, Jemma."

Her voice broke in a way that brought tears to my eyes. The door lurched behind me again. My feet skidded with a hitch of my pulse before I managed to shove it shut again. My head was starting to spin with the pain and the loss of blood. I opened my mouth to form another protest, and Olivia's eyes caught mine through the ruddy gaze.

"You promised me you wouldn't let them *use* me," she said. "Stop them. Free me. Please."

Any hope I'd been holding onto plummeted like a stone tossed into a well. All I was left with was resignation and the memory of a promise given more than ten years ago that I'd been fighting all that time to keep, a promise I'd renewed just two days ago.

Yes, I had promised her that. I hadn't wanted to fulfill that promise like this, but— *Fuck.*

Maybe I had to let go, but I couldn't just yet. "Do you

remember the good times?" I found myself saying. "When we'd get away from the others and go wandering? Searching for snakes in the shadows of the rocks. Picking flowers to chain into crowns." Petals stark white against her bright hair. I'd told her she looked like a princess.

Something glimmered in Olivia's eyes. "Of course I do," she said. "That's where I've gone every moment I could since you left. You were always here with me. You always will be. That's where I'm going to go when I leave this place—into the good times."

I didn't know if that was even possible, as nice a thought as it was. And I *hadn't* been with her, not when it had really mattered, not in the way that counted. My throat tightened. "I should have gotten here sooner. I should have gotten *there* sooner. I'm sorry, Olivia. I'm so, so sorry."

The planes of my sister's face shifted, and just for a second I saw the bright smile that had always warmed me in our childhood. I saw her, the way she was meant to be.

"I'm not sorry," she said. "This is the best I could have asked for—to die ruining their plans, with my sister guiding me along the way."

A sob sputtered out of me. "I love you," I said.

Someone bashed against the door behind me, sending me stumbling forward, but I was already raising my gun. I brought it to rest against what should have been Olivia's forehead as gently as I could, and closed my eyes with a gasp as I pulled the trigger.

The crimson light flared and snuffed out, both within Olivia's "bridge" and in the glowing lines that had stretched out into the world. In the sudden darkness, the figures who'd rammed open the door swayed uncertainly. I spun around, swaying a little myself, and put bullets in two of them just before Garrett barged into view, toppling the third with his stun gun.

I ran my fingers down my sister's form, whatever of her remained in that monstrous mess. The flesh was already chilling. She might have been dead for a long time, only the shrouded folk's energy keeping her alive. Tears dripped down my face to mingle with the blood on the floor.

I'd saved her. I'd kept my promise. I'd foiled the shrouded folk's most horrible plan. But I couldn't imagine this moment every feeling like a victory.

Could they still use her—revive her, restore her torment? My chest hitched. I couldn't take that chance.

Garrett's gaze slid past me to the mass behind me. He couldn't have made out much in the darkness, but his mouth twisted anyway.

"Is she—" he started, and didn't seem to know how to continue.

"It's over," I said. "I just need to—"

I fumbled in my pack for the flammable explosives I'd brought with me. To cover the evidence, if we needed to. Or to make sure the shrouded folk's toxic presence was burned clean from this place.

I pulled the pin from one and dropped it at the base of Olivia's mutated form. As I lurched backward, my whole body made of pain now, flames burst up, crackling over her and then across the floor in an instant.

Garrett's eyes widened at the sight of my wound. "Fucking hell, Jemma," he said, grabbing my arm. As he helped me out of the room, one last gunshot rang out, and Bash loped into view. Seeing me, the bloody mess of my clothes, and the fire raging hotter behind me with every second, his expression tensed.

"We've got to get out of here," he said, hurrying over.

"I can walk," I tried to say, but my mouth didn't move on command. My thoughts swam in my head. The last thing I was aware of was holding on to two of my lovers as they carried me from the crackling heat of my most recent act of destruction.

# CHAPTER TWENTY-THREE

*Jemma*

It felt like a very long time since I'd set foot in Sherlock and John's Baker Street apartment. Years. Perhaps decades. Although in truth it'd only been a matter of weeks.

As always, the place smelled like the smoke from Sherlock's pipe, which he was enjoying right now in the armchair across from me. John had set out a box of donuts on the table, with a meaningful glance at me that said they were for my benefit, although Garrett had taken one as well.

I leaned forward carefully in my chair to grab a cinnamon sugar one. The bullet wound on my thigh was all patched up now, but still a little raw. I'd discovered a couple days ago that if I moved too quickly, that area would start to throb all over again.

Bash, who'd barely left my side since we'd left the tower in Istanbul, let his elbow rest on the arm of the sofa with his hand against my chair, as if to indicate he was right there should I need him. It wasn't as if my injury had been *that* horrible. If I hadn't spent so much time bleeding before doing anything about it, I'd have been perfectly fine.

"Just in the few days since I've been back, the task force has taken down more than two dozen of the communes," Garrett said, apparently deciding it was on him to start the discussion. "The reactions my colleagues abroad have reported sound… promising."

"There haven't been any more bombings or shootings related to the cult," Sherlock observed. "Is there more to it than that?"

"Yes, actually." Garret gave a puzzled frown. "Some of the reports have mentioned the cultists seeming confused or out of sorts, or even mournful. One that came in this morning mentioned some of them complaining that a 'they' had abandoned them and wondering where 'they' had gone."

"The shrouded folk?" John suggested.

"That would be my best guess. I get the impression the creatures haven't been in any sort of contact with their worshippers."

A sense of satisfaction trickled through me. It was tinged with grief and regret, but at least I knew that in saving Olivia in that horrible way, I'd saved a whole lot of other people in a much more literal sense.

"That matches what I saw in the shrouded realm," I said.

Garrett stiffened. "You traveled through again?" He shot Bash a disapproving look.

My hitman raised his hands. "I follow the orders; I

don't give them. I'd like to see you argue her out of an idea when she's set on it."

"I'm none the worse for it," I broke in, glowering at both of them. "I only passed over for a few hours this time. But it was enough to confirm—the energy the shrouded folk have been consuming and, it seems, building their 'bridge' out of has almost completely faded. The stones only had a tiny flicker, and the 'spokes' of their wheel were completely gone."

Sherlock leaned forward in his chair. "Can we conclude that this is the result of your actions in Istanbul?"

"I think so." The memory of my Olivia's distorted body, of the shot I'd had to fire and the flames I'd left her to, made my lungs clench up for a moment before I could speak again. "I think the energy in the stones was fueled at least in part by the worship here that allowed the fiends to cross over. And they must have been channeling a lot of it into my sister to try to form that permanent gateway. When she died, that energy dissipated into this world—it was lost to them. She was connected to both realms. Who knows how much slipped away without them being able to stop it?"

"Then they're shut out from this world," John said. "They can't hurt anyone or incite anyone to cause harm again."

"Maybe. For the time being." I nodded to Garrett. "Your task force's efficiency is a great help. Without the communes, they'll have no way to build up that energy again. I hope."

"We can't know for sure," he said.

"No. They crossed over to our world on their own

some time back in history. And we may not get to all the communes in time. We can't assume it's over. We should all keep watch… for the rest of our lives, really, for any sign that menace has returned."

"Naturally," Sherlock said without hesitation. The others murmured their agreement. I hadn't really thought that proposition would be the difficult part of the conversation.

"There hasn't been any fallout for your careers after the mess in Istanbul?" I asked.

"Between Sherlock and I putting our spin on the publicly known events and the upper floors of the tower gutted by the fire, there've been some disgruntled comments, but nothing that I think will be an ongoing problem," Garrett said. "Especially since the violent attacks in the city have stopped now."

Sherlock chuckled dryly. "It's easier to redirect the questions when they can hardly comprehend what went on in the first place."

"Well, at least there's that." I sank a little deeper into the cushions with some relief.

"So, with the immediate threats all conquered, how will the great Jemma Moriarty pass the rest of her time from here on?" John said in a teasing tone.

There, that was the difficult part. I took another bite of my donut, rolling the sweet doughy goodness around in my mouth before I answered. "I still have business interests to keep track of. I do feel, though, that I'd prefer to keep things much more low key and relaxed than they might have been before. It was a lot of hassle, really. You can assume I won't be involved in any indiscretions you'd feel it necessary to pursue."

I wasn't going to tell them I'd never engage in criminal

activity again. I'd just overseen a couple of deals this morning. I needed to keep some of my finances and network alive in case the shrouded folk made a return, after all. But I had a broad enough foundation that I had no need to expand on it.

"And you'll be managing those interests from London?" Sherlock asked.

It wasn't an invitation or a request. I looked around at the London trio, uncertain in a way I wasn't used to and didn't entirely like.

When we'd talked about a future together back in Istanbul, we hadn't touched on any of the specifics. Perhaps they'd rethought the commitment they'd offered now that the catastrophe was averted. Now that they'd had a little time to settle back into their regular lives that they'd been content with before I'd ever meddled with them.

"I hadn't thought that far just yet," I hedged. I wasn't going to force them to stick to their offer, even if the thought of giving up the closeness we'd come to share made me feel sick.

John glanced at Sherlock with an oddly enthusiastic expression. Sherlock smiled in response, amused but warmly enough that my uneasiness started to fade.

"I happened to hear," the detective said, "that the building next door has a flat that will be available at the end of the month. A large one, I believe quite acceptable to your needs. If you wouldn't find that to be a closer quarters than you prefer, it would certainly be useful having you so near at hand. Perhaps you could even lend a thought or two to our cases as need be."

Next door. *They* wanted me that nearby, that much a part of their lives. And there was no denying the hopefulness in Garrett's eyes as he waited for my response.

A smile of my own crossed my lips with a flutter of joy in my chest. "I think that would be quite satisfactory. I'll speak to the landlord today."

# CHAPTER TWENTY-FOUR

*Jemma*

*Several months later*

I poured more water into the glass vase with its small bouquet of lilies of the valley and paused there by the window to brush my fingertips over the delicate petals. The sweet scent drifted up to my nose.

"That bunch is still going strong, huh?" Bash said from where he'd just come out of his bedroom.

"Yes." I smiled as I gave the bouquet one last caress.

The flowers weren't exactly the same as the little white ones Olivia used to pick around the outskirts of our childhood commune, but they reminded me of those… and maybe they reminded her too. I'd been setting them out on the little table beneath the living room window like an offering since we'd moved into this apartment last autumn, and they always stayed fresh and vibrant for weeks longer than any cut flowers should naturally.

It wasn't definite proof. If some part of my sister's spirit did linger on in the world, taking pleasure from little gestures like this, she hadn't communicated with me in any clear way. But if the shrouded folk could exist, if my spirit could travel from this world to theirs without my body, then I didn't see any reason why she had to be completely gone. I was happy to keep setting out flowers for her either way.

Bash came up behind me and wrapped his arms around my waist, still a little tentative with the first contact to give me time to stop him if I didn't want the embrace. I leaned into him, absorbing the solid feel of his body against mine, reveling in the fact that I could enjoy the gesture of intimacy so easily now.

It'd taken time to completely adjust to the change in our relationship from colleagues to lovers—with each other, and with the other three men in my life—now that we weren't in the middle of a desperate struggle with malicious supernatural foes. Every now and then, I was struck by a tiny flash of panic, as if I might have made a huge mistake. But those flashes came much less frequently than they had a year ago when I'd first embarked on this path. I'd gotten practiced at ignoring them.

"Will the trio be here at the usual time?" Bash asked.

"Of course—unless some urgent case comes up, I suppose."

Bash and I had been sharing the apartment next door to Sherlock and John's from the beginning, which had also been an adjustment. I suspected our arrangement was a lot like theirs was now: a common area when we wanted each other's company and separate bedrooms when we needed our privacy—but which could be shared when we were in the mood.

I saw the other men separately here or at their apartments at least once a week, but Friday nights—often blurring into Saturday mornings—were reserved for all five of us to have dinner together and whatever else we took a mind to do. Since we'd started the tradition, work had only called away one or more of the trio a handful of times.

And today... today was special, though I wasn't entirely sure any of my men would have taken note of the fact.

Bash went out to take care of a business errand, and I showered and assembled my clothes with particular care, slipping into a dress I'd picked specifically for this occasion. The air conditioning was whirring at a low level, but the silky fabric still felt delightful against the underlying July heat. I checked on the items I'd prepared and then set the table. I trusted John to choose each week's takeout, since of my lovers he had the most appreciation for a good meal.

My heart thumped away a little faster than it normally would have for a regular Friday night dinner. I closed my eyes for a second by the table, willing my nerves to settle.

It would be fine. I'd given tonight's plans more thought than I had any recent business endeavor I'd engaged in, and the men involved in that plan were a hell of a lot less treacherous than my usual associates. I just wasn't entirely sure what reaction to expect. And that reaction meant more to me than anything had since Olivia's death.

Bash returned not long before our guests were due. Sherlock arrived first, only needing to stroll a few feet down the street. He waved his phone at me after he'd stepped inside.

"A new case has come to my attention that I think you might have an interesting perspective on. I've emailed you the specifics."

I grinned. I might still have my fingers in all sorts of not-entirely-legitimate pies, but it was a pleasure matching wits with the consulting detective even when we were on the same side—seeing how closely our theories aligned, what we each might notice that the other hadn't, who could hone in on the answer to the mystery first.

"I'll take a look tomorrow, if there's not any particular rush," I said.

"No, this one has a trail some seven years cold, so I can't imagine a day will make a great deal of difference." He settled himself onto the sofa, looking quite at home. "No need to interrupt our other activities."

I couldn't resist ambling over to curl my fingers around the collar of his well-pressed shirt and steal a kiss, as a taste of the "activities" to come.

John showed up next, laden with takeout bags and with Garrett at his heels. The detective inspector helped the former doctor set out the cartons and tubs, Indian spices tickling my nose. My mouth was already watering when we sat down to eat.

The usual sorts of conversation carried on around the table—talk of each other's latest cases, recent international news, wry observations, and the possibility of taking a trip abroad this fall. Other than the few minutes when we all confirmed, as we did every week, that we hadn't seen any reason to suspect that the shrouded folk had reinvaded our world, my attention might have strayed. I obviously wasn't participating as much as usual, because when Garrett and Bash got up to clear the table, Sherlock turned to me with his piercing gaze.

"You've got something on your mind that you haven't brought up yet," he said. "How long will we need to wait before you impart that information?"

"It's nothing unpleasant," I said quickly at John's concerned glance. "I actually—I have something for each of you. Why don't we sit down in the living room, and your wait can be over?"

I got curious looks from all of them at that statement, even Bash, who I'd managed to keep all my arrangements secret from. They sat down on the sofa and armchairs where we usually had our after-dinner conversation before the tone shifted in a more bedroom-ward direction. John took the spot next to Sherlock with a casual caress of the other man's knee that gave me a flutter of pleased warmth despite my nerves. At this point, neither of their companions so much as blinked at the show of affection.

I ducked into my room to get the four packages I'd carefully wrapped this morning. "Let's start with Sherlock, since he prompted this along," I said in as even a voice as I could manage, and handed his package to him.

He turned the gift over, no doubt able to tell it was a book in less than a second. When he eased off the paper and saw the ancient leather binding and the title embossed on the cover, though, I wasn't sure I'd ever seen him quite so surprised. His head jerked up, his eyes wide as they met mine.

"Franz Sauer's analyses of criminal psychology and pathology. I've seen it referenced but—I was under the impression there were no copies left. I always wondered…" He touched the pages reverently.

I smiled with a rush of relief that my first effort had hit the mark so well. "I know. You've mentioned it once or twice. As far as I know after doing some digging, there's only *one* copy still in existence—that one you're holding right there."

He stared at me again. "The amount it must have cost you to obtain this—"

I waved him off. "Money is not an issue—and there were favors owed that defrayed some of the cost. Just don't ask for the details of how exactly I got my hands on it."

From the awe in his expression as he cradled the book, I didn't think he was likely to get nitpicky about my methods.

I turned to John next and handed him a much smaller package. "For you, I wanted to honor the side of you that you rarely let yourself completely indulge."

He raised an amused eyebrow at me and tore open the wrapping. The box inside opened to reveal a key on a fob. When he looked at me again, I tipped my head toward the window. "It's parked outside. You probably drooled over it on your way in."

From the flicker of astonishment that crossed his face, that guess had been right. He hurried over to the front of the apartment, not bothering with his walking stick, and leaned close to the glass. A brilliant smile curled his lips.

"Sherlock's not going to thank you for that," he said, but there was no mistaking the glee in his voice.

The detective tore himself away from his adoration of his own gift for long enough to ask, "What's she done now?"

John dangled the key. "She got me a motorbike. One

of the new Ducatis." His gaze slid to me. "I never told you I admired those."

I rolled my eyes at him affectionately. "The way you drive your car, it's pretty obvious you could use another outlet for that need for speed."

He chuckled with a hint of a flush in his cheeks. "It *is* a lot."

"Don't you start thinking about the money either. It was a drop in the bucket."

Picking out something that would really matter to Garrett had been harder. I suppressed the urge to fidget after I gave him his gift, which was the largest of the bunch but perhaps not as objectively impressive.

He opened the box and paused before lifting up the piece on top, a dark silk suit jacket, gingerly as if he were afraid of ruining the fine fabric just by touching it.

"It's for the conference next month," I said. He'd been asked to speak and receive an honor for his work on the task force at a major police function where all the top brass, even the prime minister, would be present, and he'd been quietly fretting about whether he'd look up to snuff ever since he'd gotten the invitation. "If it doesn't fit quite right, I can get some more tailoring done, but I think I know your body rather well by now."

Even the prime minister was unlikely to have a suit quite that well designed, though I'd gone for understated rather than flashy in consideration of Garrett's tastes. He looked at the pants folded beneath the jacket and the gold cuff links I'd tucked into the corner in their smaller box and then back at me with a shimmer in his eyes.

"Thank you," he said. "I can't imagine it's anything but perfect already."

Bash had watched all the goings-on with bemused

interest. When I held out the last gift to him, little more than an envelope covered in gift paper, my hitman shook his head at me before he dug his thumb under the folds. "You know I've already got everything I could want, Mori."

"I know you *could* have everything you want," I said. "But you have a bad habit of putting what you think I need over what you do."

Before he could question that comment, two plane tickets were falling out of the envelope into his hands. He blinked at them for a few seconds as understanding washed over his face. "Jemma," he started, and then didn't seem to know how to go on.

"I can spare you for two weeks," I said. "You've been talking to your brother and sister for almost a year now—it's time you got to see them again, properly. Or if I've been mistaken and you'd *really* rather not, we can exchange them for a trip to Fiji or wherever. But you won't be with me in London for those two weeks. You deserve a break, too."

He managed to keep his expression relatively impassive, but I heard the emotion in his voice. "Well, if you insist… Thank you."

John glanced around at the other men, still lit up with excitement over his own gift. "Why all this now, Jemma? There's still five more months until Christmas."

My gaze lifted to Sherlock, who I figured was the one most likely to connect the dots if any of them did. His small smile in return told me he already had.

"It's exactly one year since the day in Rio de Janeiro when we all agreed to join forces with Jemma to tackle the shrouded folk," he said. "The anniversary of our official partnership?"

"That sounds like a reasonable way to put it," I said.

Garrett had closed the box with his suit, his arms resting on it in a protective stance. "I didn't realize—we don't have anything for you."

My throat constricted, but my heart only pounded harder. My heart that had felt so inaccessible for so long, with no room in it for anything except my sister and the vengeance I meant to deal out for her.

My love for her, and the pain and grief that came with it, hadn't shrunk. No, that wasn't it at all. What I'd felt over the past year had been more as if my heart were growing, bit by bit, to have more and more capacity for affection and devotion with every day I spent with these men.

I swallowed hard. "You've given me so much. For months, you've all offered me your love when I couldn't respond in kind, when I wasn't sure I ever would be able to... So in a way, I've kept you waiting a very long time for this. It seemed only fair to show it as well as say it."

Even though I was sure of them, even though I'd planning for days how I'd say them, the words stuck before I could propel them out of my mouth. "I love you. All of you. There isn't any way I'd rather spend the rest of my life than what we have now."

The flash of panic hit me, for what I hoped would be the last time. In that instant, I couldn't look at any of them. Someone sucked in a breath, and then all four of my lovers were getting to their feet, surrounding me, wrapping me up in a joint embrace. They didn't need to say the words back right then for me to know they felt the same.

I was Jemma Moriarty, devoted sister, cult escapee, criminal mastermind, attached beyond what I could ever have believed to these four incredible men. Our arrangement might have looked odd to outside eyes, but what any outsider thought didn't matter. It worked perfectly for us. And it was far more of a happy ending than I'd ever believed could be mine.

Eva Chase lives in Canada with her family. She loves stories both swoony and supernatural, and strong women and the men who appreciate them. Along with the Moriarty's Men series, she is the author of the Looking Glass Curse trilogy, the Their Dark Valkyrie series, the Witch's Consorts series, the Dragon Shifter's Mates series, the Demons of Fame Romance series, the Legends Reborn trilogy, and the Alpha Project Psychic Romance series.

*Connect with Eva online:*
www.evachase.com
eva@evachase.com